Deliriously Happy

Deliriously
Happy

LARRY DOYLE

ecco
ANNIVERSARY
40

An Imprint of HarperCollinsPublishers

The following pieces were originally published in the *New Yorker*: Fun Times!; Me v. Big Mike; Sleeper Camp; May We Tell You Our Specials This Evening?; Disengagements; Life Without Leann: A Newsletter; Portrait in Evil: My Story; Adventures in Experimentation; I Killed Them in New Haven; Stop Me If You've Heard This One; Notes on My Next Bestseller; Let's Talk About My New Movie; Last of the Cro-Magnons*; Why We Strike; We Request the Honor of Your Presence at GywnnandDaveShareTheirJoy.com; Bad Dog; What Am I Going to Do with My Mega Millions?; Please Read Before Suing; I'm Afraid I Have Some Bad News; Is There a Problem Here?; You Won't Have Nixon to Kick Around Anymore, Dirtbag. In *Esquire*: Me: An Introduction*; My Heart: My Rules; You Asked for It*; The Larry Doyle Story As Told to Larry Doyle; An Open Letter to All Academy Members, Creative Artists, and Anyone Else Who Still Believes in Freedom of Expression; The Babyproofer; Freezer Madness. In the *National Lampoon*: Dating Tips*; Ask the Eight Ball; Are You Insane?; Media Culpa; Local Wag*; The Rest of the Story; Huck of Darkness; Then What?; Recent Supreme Court Decisions*; How to Handle Your Money*. On Popcornfiction.com: Whacking the Baby; Thank You for Considering My Cult. In *Tin House*: Freelance File. In *Kugelmass*: Eulogy for Bob. (*In a slightly, significantly, or dramatically different form.)

FIRST EDITION

Designed by Suet Yee Chong

Library of Congress Cataloging-in-Publication Data has been applied for.

ISBN 978-0-06-196683-5

11 12 13 14 15   OV/RRD   10 9 8 7 6 5 4 3 2 1

For Julia Just

The Eight Ages of Happiness

HIGH SPIRITS

MERRIMENT

BLISS

ACCEPTANCE

RAPTURE

PIECES LEFT OUT OF THIS COLLECTION

Me: An Introduction

The first thing you need to know about me is you're standing too close. Put the book down and take a couple steps back, all right, friend?

It's for your own good. I am a man of powerful opinions, requiring strong gestures and sudden movements to make known, and I wouldn't want to see you hospitalized unnecessarily.

If you know me—which you don't, so don't pretend to your friends that you do, until you've read further—you know one thing: I'm against the war. As this volume goes to press, that includes all those Muslim wars, which I'm counting as one war. If some new wars have started in the last couple of weeks, I'm against those as well. I opposed the Vietnam War as a baby, and I believe I would have opposed the Korean War; I'll have to look it up someday and find out. Had I been around, I definitely would have opposed WWII. In hindsight, you can say it turned out all right, but we'll never really know how many lives could have been saved had we given appeasement a chance.

Nevertheless, I'm not an anti-Semite. I am an anti-anti-Semite. Unless that makes me a Semite. Then I'm something else.

Another thing about me: I support gay rights, even though I'm not gay, personally or professionally. Or secretly. I mean, I'm so heterosexual I can't even masturbate. But I believe whatever two guys want to do with each other's parts is fine, as long as I'm not in the room, and two gals as well, even if I am.

Also, I won't eat anything with a face that might recognize me. Neither will I eat anything with a name, be it Elsie, or Beauty, or Old Red. If I must eat an animal, I insist on being led to believe it died humanely, preferably by its own hand. I eat a lot of lemming (tastes like vole).

I won't wear fur on purpose. I believe Fur Is Murder, on account of the clever internal rhyme.

As far as evolution goes, I don't buy it. If chimpanzees are our closest living relatives, sharing more than 98 percent of our DNA, you should be able to mate with them, but you can't. You really can't. I have a theory that we are evolved from cows and sheep, but I can't go into the details right now. It's in peer review.

Oh, and global warming is our single greatest challenge today, I believe. Along with fresh water. Plus religious extremism and renewable energy. And AIDS babies, natch. Yeah, sure, oppression of women/breast cancer, too. Those are all our single greatest challenges today. This I believe.

Of course what I believe doesn't matter. You just wasted a lot of time there. Because I'm a man of action. What I do is who I am, and I do a lot.

I don't carry cash, but if I did I would certainly share my hard-earned money with panhandlers and vagrants and the like. In lieu of payment, I offer smart career advice and motivational sayings.

For the past couple of years I've Gone Zero, as many big celebrities are doing. To reduce my carbon emissions, I've carved my name on that tree over there, and several others around the neighborhood. There's also this moss growing across my back and down my legs. I have to face south all the time, but I think our planet is worth it.

I recycle constantly. I eat out of garbage cans whenever there's nobody with a whisk broom around. I am also progressing in my goal of achieving zero net biomass. Hence the jars. The technology is not yet there to turn our urine into gasoline and excrement into some other wonderful thing, but when it is, I'll be ready. Also, it's not easy to fart into jars, but I'm getting good at it.

I don't wear hats. This is not a hat. It is my hair, woven into a porkpie. There's a difference.

When you invite me to your next dinner party, you should know that in addition to the above, I am conversant in the following topics: funny Bill Murray movies. And fair warning: if you seat me next to a precocious, talkative child, there will be punching.

Joy

Fun Times!

Do your kids like to have fun?

Come to Fun Times!*

Do you like to watch your kids having fun?

Bring 'em to Fun Times!

Are your kids sullen, withdrawn, wearing a lot of black lately, and you, your life practically over, and for what?

For gosh sakes, get the whole family down to Fun Times!

Fun Times!'s "fine amusement dining" is the most fun you can have, legally, in the United States right now. Why spend thousands of dollars flying to Disney World when you can spend less than half of that indoors and malaria-free, within a day's drive of most cities?

To find the Fun Times! nearest you, simply get on your favor-

---

* Fun Times!, formerly Fun Tymes, is not affiliated with Ye Olde Fun Tymes or the New York Times Company, and does not recognize their debts or financial obligations.

ite highway and keep going until you hear the fun! Park in any of our outer lots and hop on the Jolly Trolley,[†] or walk on ahead if you prefer. Once you've reached the Fun Times! intake office, you will be asked to fill out a few simple waivers and financial disclosure forms.

You're moments away from fun!

Next you'll purchase your children's Fun Times! Happy Cards!, which can be loaded in twenty-dollar increments by Grumpy McPoops, or set to Unlimited Happiness! for kids whose parents would prefer to spend the money now, rather than later on therapy and make-goods.

You're on the cusp of fun!

Release the children!

The first thing you'll want to do upon entering the Fun Times! Game Dome is stagger over to the Grown-Up Pagoda and purchase a pair of ear plugs. They cost a little more, but we recommend Westone ES49s, the kind Pete Townshend uses to preserve what's left of his hearing.

Now take a look around.[‡] Was there ever anything this much fun when you were a kid?

Maybe there was, and your parents lied to you about it.

But you're not them, and you don't have to be them.

Just one look into your children's glowing, jittery eyes will tell you how much cooler you are than they ever were.

That may not happen right away, but rest assured your kids are in here somewhere, enjoying video-game graphics almost as good as the ones at home. While you're waiting, why not check out

---

[†] The Jolly Trolley is not operated by the Fun Times! Company, which makes no warrants as to its driver, Glenn, or to the final destination of the Trolley.

[‡] Epileptics should not take a look around.

our costumed entertainment? We are proud to host the Medi-Cools, a cartoon menagerie developed by Hanna-Barbera for the National Institutes of Health in the seventies. Feel free to arm wrestle with Mike O'Cardial or shake hands with Whiz and Wee, the Kidney Twins, because, for the most part, the children won't go near them.[§]

Don't bother yelling; your kids can't hear you.

Maybe you should eat something. There's a restaurant in here, too, in the direction of the smell. For the little ones, we have pizza, fries, and chicken shapes. And, for you, six sizes of beer!

We strongly advise against searching for your kids down the Console Canyons; they'll find their way out long before you do. What we recommend is that you pick one place and stand there.

But not there!

You've been Goob™ed!

Don't worry, that was gallons and gallons of totally "natural" fun,[**] which won't ruin any fabric developed after 2005. That slight burning sensation is not humiliation, so relax and enjoy the laughter of hundreds of children, all because of you!

And, look: here come your kids now, laughing like they've never laughed before, and apparently unharmed. They just want you to hold on to the six hundred game tickets they've accumulated so far—almost halfway to a Frog Clacker!—and then they're gone again, into the fun.

Did they call back, "I love you, Dad," as they slipped into the neon darkness? We think they did.

[§] Ladies, please note: Dr. Lungtissue is not a licensed physician.

[**] Goob™ is a proprietary peanut-based gel, which may contain traces of peanuts and whole peanuts still in the shell. People who are sensitive to peanuts and/or tree nuts should have read the waiver more carefully.

He was the end of my pompom. I'm the cheerleader.

—Remark made by former Disney chairman Michael Eisner about
his protégé, Jeffrey Katzenberg, as revealed in court proceedings.

$60 zillion.

—Amount of settlement suggested by Mr. Katzenberg's attorney,
as quoted in the *Hollywood Reporter*

Me v. Big Mike

**Now comes the Plaintiff, Larry Doyle, and for his First Complaint
against the Defendant states unto the Honorable Court as follows:**

1. That the Defendant, BIG MIKE, was at all times relevant to the
    above-entitled cause of action, a student in the fourth grade at

St. Mary's Elementary School in Buffalo Grove, in the County of Cook, State of Illinois.

2. That the Defendant, BIG MIKE, was also known as BAD MIKE, BIG BAD MIKE, MIKE THE GIANT, GIANT MIKE, THE JOLLY GREEN MIKE, MIKE THE MIDGET KILLER, and THE POUNDER.

3. That the Defendant was then, and has remained, large for his age.

4. That the Defendant is now the owner and operator of BIG MIKE'S ACURA, in Palatine, in the County of Cook, State of Illinois.

5. That the Defendant, at all times relevant to the above-entitled cause of action, controlled the fourth grade through a reign of terror in his capacity as Bully.

6. That the Plaintiff served the Defendant in the capacity of Sidekick, from approximately September 11, 1967, until November 13, 1967.

7. That on or about May 19, 1999, the Plaintiff recovered memories of unimaginable conscious pain and suffering inflicted by the Defendant, as well as of a breach of contract.

8. That recovered memories, as are those of the Plaintiff, are recognized as real and legitimate by several hypnotherapy and anti-satanic cult groups, and have become an instrument of standard legal practice in the circumvention of statutory limitations in the filing of lawsuits (*cf. Roseanne v. Everybody*).

9. That the amount in controversy exceeds the jurisdictional amount of Ten Thousand Dollars ($10,000.00), and that the amount of Plaintiff's damages in this case exceed Sixty Zillion Dollars ($60,000,000,000,000 . . . *etc.*)

COUNT I

Intentional infliction of emotional distress, physical intimidation, extortion, and bodily injury on the part of Defendant.

10. That on or about September 11, 1967, the Defendant chose the Plaintiff from among several candidates to be his sole and exclusive Sidekick.

11. That the said Plaintiff understood or was made to understand that his Duties as sole and exclusive Sidekick to the Defendant would include but not be limited to: establishing and maintaining the Defendant's reputation for violence; taunting the smaller, weaker, or more infirm of the students under the Defendant's purview; scheduling Poundings on behalf of the Defendant; collecting milk and other monies on behalf of the Defendant; seconding the Defendant's remarks, laughing at his jokes and insults, and otherwise bolstering the Defendant's self-confidence.

12. That the Plaintiff was led to believe that by performing these Duties he would be exempt from the reign of terror visited upon the fourth grade by the Defendant. In fact, despite the Plaintiff's best efforts to fulfill his Duties in a competent and timely manner, the Defendant focused a majority of his Bullying activities on the person of the Plaintiff.

13. That the Defendant did intentionally and maliciously inflict emotional distress on the Plaintiff, in the following particulars, by way of illustration, and not limitation:

    a. Intentionally and maliciously subjecting the Plaintiff to ridicule by frequently alluding to the Plaintiff's then small stature, applying to the Plaintiff such appellations as Shrimpo, Tiny Tim, Jr., Butt-Munchkin, and Knee-high to a Grasshopper Turd;

b. Intentionally and maliciously humiliating the Plaintiff by requiring him to answer to the name Midge, a shortened form of Midget, in a high, girlish register, under threat of a Pounding;

c. Intentionally and maliciously defaming the Plaintiff with the creation and performance of a mock television program, sometimes entitled *I Hate Larry* and at other times known as *That Little Midget*, which involved the Defendant's walking on his knees while producing flatulence sounds with his mouth, said portrayal being an inaccurate and slanderous depiction of the Plaintiff;

d. On several occasions, in front of peers, drawing attention to the Plaintiff's "boner" when none was present.

14. That on or about September 30, 1967, Defendant conscripted the Plaintiff, on a Saturday, outside and beyond the terms of his employment as a playground Sidekick, into indentured servitude in the building of a Fort in the backyard of the Defendant. On this occasion, and with no provocation, the Defendant flung with extreme force the Plaintiff's father's good hammer into Poo Pond, so named for its adjacency to a sewage treatment plant. The Defendant then ridiculed the Plaintiff for his subsequent uncontrolled weeping, fostering in the Plaintiff an inability to cry as an adult, limiting his emotional range and diminishing his enjoyment of romantic motion pictures and other popular entertainment.

15. That while the Plaintiff was solely responsible for scheduling Poundings on behalf of the Defendant, and conscientiously ar-

ranged for such Poundings to occur after school hours or during recess, the Defendant nevertheless did inflict innumerable unscheduled, impromptu, and unprovoked Poundings on the Plaintiff. These Poundings, which ranged in severity from Sluggings to Pummelings, were visited upon the Plaintiff for such minor infractions as insufficient milk money collection, looking at the Defendant askance, and failure to schedule another Pounding for that day.

16. That by way of extreme and outrageous conduct the Defendant visited ritual tortures upon the Plaintiff, including Indian Burns, Dutch Rubs, Pink Bellies, Wet Willies, Noogies, and, completely without regard to sanitation and safety, Swirlees, in which the Plaintiff's head was forced deep into the bowl of a toilet, which was then flushed, causing the toilet water to swirl about the Plaintiff's head and face in an alarming manner.

17. That on or about November 13, 1967, the Plaintiff's ninth birthday, Defendant said he had "a special present" for the Plaintiff but in fact used the occasion to commit a deliberate and heinous act on the Plaintiff. Reaching into the Plaintiff's trousers from behind, the Defendant gripped the elastic waistband of the Plaintiff's briefs and yanked upward with a violent motion. Yelling, "I'm a cheerleader! You are my pompom," the Defendant did wantonly and recklessly raise the Plaintiff into the air, supported solely by his briefs, and proceeded to thrust his arm out violently several times under the pretext of giving the Plaintiff "birthday cheers." As a direct result of this assault, the Plaintiff was transferred from St. Mary's to a public school, where he received an inferior education.

COUNT IV

Breach of contract on the part of Defendant.

18. That the Defendant stated on several occasions that the Plaintiff, for his services as Sidekick, would receive "his share" of milk and other monies collected.

19. That on the sole occasion the Plaintiff inquired about his afore-mentioned share he received payment in the form of a Pounding.

20. That the Plaintiff estimates that he collected no less than Seven Dollars and Twenty Cents ($7.20) on behalf of the Defendant.

21. That Ten Percent (10%) being a reasonable "share," based on es-tablished show-business practice, the Plaintiff was then entitled to Seventy-Two Cents ($0.72). With interest of Six Percent (6%) per annum, and irrespective of any compensation due the Plain-tiff as a result of the conscious pain, fright, shock, and anxiety then caused and mental pain, anguish, and sorrow which con-tinue to be caused by the Defendant's actions, Plaintiff is now owed Four Dollars and Sixty-Five Cents ($4.65).

My Pet Store

Big, happy dogs, not yippy rat dogs or saggy, sad dogs.

Permapup, a medication that keeps your puppy from developing into a full-grown dog.

All the monkeys allowed by law.

Celebrity fish.

A discount spider bin: one dollar buys you all the spiders you can grab in thirty seconds.

Only the most delicious rabbits.

Petsicle Maker, a home frozen sperm bank that inexpensively preserves your pet's genes should you reconsider after cutting his nuts off.

Gerbils crossbred with phosphorescent algae so they glow in the dark and can be caught more easily when they inevitably escape.

Fur Doo, a pet grooming service that gives your pet the same haircut you have.

Hawks painted to look like friendly parrots.

Really big snakes.

Community Outreach to reduce the number of stray or annoying cats roaming the neighborhood (see above).

We are under the impression that C. views our ownership of the house as a deviation from the original purpose of our mission here. We'd like to assure you that we do remember what it is. From our perspective, purchase of the house was solely a natural progression of our prolonged stay here. It was a convenient way to solve the housing issue, plus to "do as the Romans do" in a society that values home ownership.

—Accused spies Richard and Cynthia Murphy to their Russian contact, from the federal criminal complaint

Sleeper Camp

Jul 25

Drop-off went according to plan. I've secured a bed in élite Cabin Eight [$50, gratuity] to better observe alpha camper R., as instructed. I am at present in a lower bunk, and will need to gain an upper berth to have access to the high-level talks that occur up there after lights-out.

A tense moment at First Fire. During the recital of Greasy Grimy Gopher Guts, I sang "little dirty birdie feet" instead of the local perversion, "chopped up baby parakeet." My error was pointed out by E., an overweight boy seeking to deflect negative attention from himself. My response, that E. had not heard me correctly due to the obstruction of his piglike ears with fatty fat, made E. cry, provoking hard laughter amongst the others. The head counselor gave me a demerit for poor sportsmanship, which is sure to put me in good stead with the most important campers.

To the greater glory of Sleeping Bear!

Jul 26

After only one day, I've isolated a crucial factor in Screaming Eagle's continued dominance at All-Lake: the breakfasts are amazing! The eggs are fresh, not powdered military surplus; the bacon crumbles warm and chewy, not chemical pellets. There's at least seven varieties of sweet roll—soft with no discernable insect parts—fresh fruit, and a nearly endless selection of brand-name cereals served with whole, reduced-fat, skim, and even soy milk upon request! If we were to institute such a hearty regimen, I believe our performance at All-Lake would dramatically improve, and there would be fewer swoonings.

After lunch (all-beef burgers with a choice of real cheese!), I was hog-tied on the orders of R. and stowed under my bunk, and thus am unable to report on the afternoon's activities. My fears for the mission were allayed by counselor K., who heard my strategic whimpering and freed me before afternoon snack (pineapple on the husk!). He explained that the bondage and humiliation of new mates is a tradition in Cabin Eight and signifies my initiation into the group. Objective achieved.

To solidify my newfound position, following dinner (chicken cutlets—all white meat!) I treated R. to his choice of ice creams at Canteen [$24, entertainment]. He sampled several, tossing them unfinished to the ground, before settling on a Choco-Taco similar to his first selection. The obese E. watched us with growing fury. He may have to be neutralized.

On a separate but related matter, I wonder whether we might devise a better mode of exchange. It's difficult to find fresh animal scat, especially after dark, and the monies I retrieved from your last drop raised questions at the Canteen. The designated old oak has several hollows and crannies that might equally suffice, I respectfully suggest.

Jul 27

I am under the impression that C. views my stay here as an indulgence, and that I'm being corrupted by bourgeois "treats." I'd like to assure you that I remain committed to our goal of crushing Camp Screaming Eagle at the next All-Lake, and that I partake of their superior cuisine and comforts merely to not arouse suspicion. I would happily share a single desiccated carob biscuit with my Sleeping Bear brethren than partake in the whole of the Sundae Bar promised us this Thursday.

Now, if we've put that matter to rest, I am pleased to report a small but significant victory. Utilizing the warm-water torture technique from training, I induced L., my bunkmate, to micturate in his sleep. Having previously obtained an extra set of clean sheets [$20, laundry], I traded these and my silence for L.'s superior berth. I'm an Upper!

During archery today it became evident that Screaming Eagle would again take this event, and no wonder: their instructor is Park Sung-Hyun, the three-time Olympic gold medalist! I mean no disrespect to Captain F., our long-serving Survival Arts instructor, but it's surprising how much can be accomplished in an hour session uninterrupted by digressions about ATF agents and former wives who may or may not be ATF agents.

I purchased Northwoods Canvas Utility Pants, Merrell Chameleon Gore-Tex Ventilator Hikers, Barz Cross-Sport Goggles, and an L.L. Bean Neoprene Wet Suit, from the camp's pro shop, on the advice of R. [$289, equipment/camouflage]. These will allow me to move inconspicuously amongst the other campers, some of whom have made note of my attire. At morning roundup, fat E. commented cryptically that I "looked like something the *bear* dragged in." I was forced to savagely pink-belly him as a diversion.

Jul 28

My infiltration of the upper sleeping echelon is paying dividends, well worth the additional outlay to Counselor K. to overlook bunk seniority regulations [$60, gratuities]. Last night R. regaled us for more than an hour after lights-out, artfully melding terrifying stories with ribald sounds, and then, as we were falling asleep, he quietly revealed the depressing familial circumstances that have resulted in his summer-long stays at Screaming Eagle, which he referred to as his "real home." Then he farted to great effect.

Jul 29

I do remember why I am here.

Nevertheless, nothing of value was learned today.

In consideration of our previous communication, I only made two trips to the Sundae Bar this evening.

Jul 30

Despite strong reservations, I carried out the attack tonight precisely as directed. I am unable to report success.

While I did manage to replace the one hundred Hershey's bars with Ex-Lax [$500, explosives] before the Great Bonfire, the rigged s'mores were quickly detected by the lardy E., who knows his chocolate. He attempted to blame me, having amassed an impressive dossier, including a murky cell-phone video of me inadvertently singing "Hail, Screaming Bear" at Sundown. (It's the same melody, and I was loopy on tiramisu!) R. rose to my defense and, invoking the smelt-it/dealt-it rule, accused E. of the sabotage, and of being fat. The missing chocolate was found in E.'s footlocker, of course, and he took quite a beating.

Unfortunately, in the end, the Screaming Eagles, rather than being drained and debilitated on the eve of All-Lake, have emerged revitalized and determined to exact vengeance. And so it is with great regret that I must inform you that we're going to totally kick your butts tomorrow.

Armchair Father

When I came down for breakfast that morning—Thursday morning—Dad was there in his chair in front of the TV room TV, asleep, or as it turned out, dead I guess. This wasn't what you would call out of the ordinary, I mean him sleeping, except for the fact that the TV was showing some California beach guys playing volleyball, which wasn't one of Dad's sports, though he had been getting a lot less picky these last few months. I remember once I got up to get some juice or Coke to drink—it was pretty late—and Dad was in there in his chair, half awake, watching a woman demonstrate how to turn your old dungarees into high-fashion designer jeans with something called a Gemm Gunn. And we have cable, so it wasn't like it was the only thing on or anything.

Anyway, I turned the TV off on my way out to school, and when I got home it was back on, so the fact that Dad was asleep again wasn't what you would call suspicious. But what was suspicious was that my sister Moll was in there, sitting on Dad's lap, watching *The Ping-Pong and Foamy Show.* That was weird because Dad hates puppets in the first place, and especially weird in the second place because Dad had been pretty much a total grump since his unemployment ran out, and didn't place a high priority on family togetherness like he once did.

—Hey, Roundbaby, you better hope he doesn't wake up, I said to Molly. She put her finger to her lips, like to say *shh* to me, but instead she had her finger turned the wrong way around, like to button her own lip. She grabbed a hold of Dad's old blue robe and cuddled up, pushing her head in close to his chest; then she turned to me and stuck out her tongue. Kind of sick, now that I think about it afterward.

I made Molly and me dinner, and then when Mom came home from work, I asked her if she wanted me to wake Dad up. (Mostly because my favorite show, *Operation: U.S.A.,* was about to start and Dad refused to have it on if he was in the room.) But Mom just made that partway smile she sometimes makes.

—Leave your father alone, she said. He's had a hard day.

So I had to watch TV upstairs on the dinky TV, which sucked.

The next morning, which was Friday now, Dad was still asleep in his chair in the TV room, with the TV blasting *Sea Monkeys* cartoons, which even Moll doesn't watch. I was late for soccer practice, though, so I didn't think about it too much until I got back home and Dad was still asleep in the exact same position in the chair, watching *Chia Pet Adventures,* yet with Moll nowhere in sight. I knew then something was wrong. I turned off the TV, and that's when I noticed that Dad wasn't snoring like usual.

—Dad. *Dad,* I said. But Dad didn't say anything.

I went over and shook him. The remote fell out of his hand to the floor, but his fingers stayed in their remote-controller positions.

I told Molly to go to her room when she came in, and when she asked why, I screamed at her and she cried. Mom didn't come home for another two hours, and I spent the whole time standing in the TV room, staring at Dad, hoping he would move or do something.

—Mom, Dad isn't moving, I told Mom when she got home.

—Newsflash, Mom said.

—He hasn't moved since yesterday.

—Oh, for godsakes, my Mom said, stomping out of the kitchen to the TV room. Brian, this has got to, a, you're scaring the children now.

Mom shook Dad, a lot harder than I did, but it didn't change Dad at all. She yanked Dad by his arm, and then she froze.

—Great, great, she said, slapping the back of Dad's hand real hard. She grabbed Dad around the wrist, fumbling with it for a few seconds, before letting Dad fall back into the chair, into his usual position.

Mom stood there, looking at Dad, like I did, for the longest time, without saying anything. And then she started laughing; and then she started crying, still laughing; and then she told me to go get Moll and pack up to go to Grandmom's for the weekend.

When we came back on Sunday night, Dad was still in his

chair, which gave me the creeps right off, big-time. Dad was sitting straight up, with his eyes closed and this super calm expression on his face, like back when he used to meditate. He was wearing the velvety red-and-black robe Mom had given him for Father's Day a couple of years ago, which he never wore because he said the one he had, the blue one, was all broken in. In his hand he had a remote control, but not the one from the TV room TV, but from our old TV broken down in the basement. Dad's thumb was hovering right over the channel-changer button. His hair was combed, and it looked like he had a tan.

—So, what do you guys think? Mom asked. Doesn't your father look nice in that robe?

—It's a pretty robe, Mommy, Moll said.

Mom was standing behind me, with her fingers rubbing the top part of my chest, making little circles.

—What do *you* think, Stephan?

I said the only thing I could think of: He smells funny.

—That's just the potpourri, honey. It won't be so strong in a couple days. So, you kids, want to order a pizza?

—Yay! Molly said.

—We had a lot to eat at Grandma's, I said. I'm not hungry. I have an algebra test tomorrow. I better go study.

I actually didn't eat much at all at Grandma's—which Grandma made a big deal about, taking my temperature all the time—but I did have an algebra test. I didn't study for it, though. I kept trying to think of everything, but none of it would sit still in my head; I couldn't even get it in the right order. I just lay in my bed, staring, getting hungrier and hungrier.

I felt sick the next morning and I didn't want to go to school, but I didn't want to stay home either, so I went. I felt dizzy all day, probably on account of the fact that I didn't eat any breakfast, and also everything that happened. I wanted to tell my friend Gregory all about it, but I figured he wouldn't understand and I couldn't explain it to him either. Whenever my parents used to do something weird like this, they always said I'd understand when I got older, but I'll bet that won't happen in this case. I'm sure everybody thought I was acting weird.

When I got home, Moll was there with some of her friends, playing in the TV room with Dad, which I didn't think was a good idea but she said Mom said it was okay, which, at that point, sounded like something Mom would say. They were all in the TV room, all giggles and squeals, taking turns sitting on Dad, and I couldn't deal with that so I went up to my room. Well, before not too long, I heard all this shrieking and so I came back down. What happened was they were horsing around on Dad and tipped him out of his chair, knocking some of the stuffing out of him. I sent them all home, and that night Emily Barton woke up shrieking and the next morning the police came and took Dad away.

The police asked me where my mom was and I said she was at work, and they asked me where she worked and I wouldn't tell them, but they found her anyway.

Uncle Tim came to stay with us while Mom talked things over with the police. It turned out that they had to let her go after forty-eight hours, since they couldn't find any major crimes to charge her with. The TV made a lot of jokes about that, and not just on the local shows. One famous talk-show guy told a joke about how the police finally decided the only crime they could charge my mom with was practicing taxidermy without a license.

Uncle Tim wouldn't tell me what taxidermy was, so I looked it up in the dictionary. It was an okay joke, I guess. Another guy made a joke about how they weren't going to charge my mom, but they decided to arrest my dad for impersonating a congressman. I didn't get it. Uncle Tim laughed, but then he saw me and stopped.

I told him he didn't have to not laugh, but he turned off the TV and came over and put his hand on my shoulder, like Dad used to when he had something he thought was important to tell me. Uncle Tim told me that sometimes people laugh when things are so horrible they can't cry, which is something Mom told me once too, so maybe it's sort of a family saying.

Anyway, after keeping my mom for forty-eight hours and not having any crimes to arrest her for, the police had to let her go. I watched it on TV. Mom was walking out of the police station with our lawyer, Uncle Chuck (he's not a real uncle), when she was surrounded by all these reporters who were shoving microphones and things at her. One of the reporters kept yelling out, *Why'd you do it? Why'd you do it?* Finally my mom quit trying to push through them and stopped in middle of all the microphones.

—Can you tell us why you did it? the reporter asked again.

That kind of partway smile came on Mom's face again. She said: I think it's important to have a man in the house.

When Mom got home, she went right to bed and took Moll with her.

Uncle Tim says I'll have to be the man of the house now, because no matter what Mom says, there's no way they're going to give Dad back. I don't know about that. Later that night I snuck down to the TV room to see if we made the eleven o'clock news, and it was like Dad was still there, sitting in his chair, as always. His chair still had his dent; it was deep and shaped exactly like him, fresh still, like he had just gotten out of it to go to the bathroom or something, and I was afraid that if I sat in his spot, he'd be back in a few seconds to yell at me to get out. It's like Mom used to say: Dad made a pretty big impression on that chair.

Ecstasy

Dating Tips

First dates can be an uncomfortable experience for both parties, but here are a few things you can do to make it a fun, interesting experience for all.

Spit into a handkerchief every fifteen minutes or so.

If your date relates a particularly stiff anecdote, say, "That reminds me of a story," and proceed to relate the *exact same anecdote,* only substituting yourself for your date in the story.

Don't talk with your mouth full of blood.

Driving home, nervously glance in the rearview mirror and say, "Shit, it's Mom. Hold on tight while I try to lose her."

At the end of the date, tell your date you had a perfectly wonderful evening, while pressing a dollar bill into his or her hand.

May We Tell You Our Specials This Evening?

We have several.

For an appetizer, the chef has prepared a slaughter of baby salmon on toast points of nine grains—blue corn, barley, rye, chaff, stover, found rice, horse-rolled oats, balsa, and fermented teff flown in daily from Ethiopia—and fancy assorted nuts, which may contain up to ten percent peanuts. The salmon is very fresh; it was hatched just this morning.

The chef is also offering a personal favorite, his hot spiced rocks. These are igneous and sedimentary varietals, half-washed and heated to nine hundred degrees Fahrenheit, then gleefully sprinkled with international peppers.

For the more adventurous, we have a selection of freshly pur-chased water crackers spread with unmarked pastes, jellies, and unguents found in our kitchen.

We are also featuring a tasting gavage, in which every ap-petizer on the menu is wheeled to your table and forced down the gullets of two to four people. The price is twenty-eight dollars per person, plus a nominal service charge. To accompany this course, the chef recommends a bottle of the Pete, which is quite sneaky tonight. It comes in cherry or mixed berry, and is served in brown paper.

Our special soup tonight is Georgian alligator turtle, prepared and presented in its own shell. This soup is served cold and slimy, and, in the traditional manner, with the head and legs attached. We recommend that you not touch the head, as it can snap your finger clean off before you can say, "Hey, this turtle is still alive."

In addition to our usual salad, our chef has prepared a faux tuna Niçoise, which he is recommending not be eaten by anyone trying to limit their mercury consumption.

We also have an iceberg lettuce leaf, wetted and centered on the plate.

With your soup and salad, the chef suggests two or three cocktails, and not cosmopolitans or candy martinis but real men's drinks. He is recommending a very interesting Thai vodka he managed to get into this country; the "liquor" is chilled into an aspic, spooned into a shot glass, then served between the breasts of Alicia over there.

Before I tell you the entrées, there is one change to the menu: we are out of the pan-fried squirrel brains tonight, as our supplier fell out of a tree this morning.

Our fish is a Blue Happy, which is a euphemism. It is mostly filleted and sunbaked, then disinfected and served with what may or may not be capers. Blowholes can be requested for an additional charge.

The pasta is a single, comically long strand of spaghetti with a surprise at the end. The sauce is of no consequence.

And, finally, tonight we are offering a very special entrée that has been the subject of much debate in the kitchen. It is roast loin of Oliver, a pig that our chef has raised since infancy. Oliver was the runt in a litter of nine, and was, as you can see in this picture, bottle-fed by the chef as a young boy. Oliver grew strong and proud and was soon beating his siblings in their rutting games. Extremely smart, Oliver thrice saved our chef from fires caused by careless smoking. However, in his latter years Oliver has grown bitter and incontinent, and just yesterday he ate the chef's brand-new iPhone.

Once we receive our first order this evening, Oliver will be smothered by a pillow filled with virgin goose down. This may take the chef some time. Oliver will then be hacked to pieces and charbroiled on a specially blessed grill. His loin will then be laid to rest on a bed of tears, with asparagus and a confit of something. The chef would like to serve Oliver to you personally, and deliver a short eulogy. He will remain tableside, drinking steadily as you eat in silence. Because of the singular nature of this dish and its extreme emotional cost, it is priced at eighteen thousand dollars.

Would you like to order now, or do you need a few moments?

Date with an Angel[*]

I've been to this restaurant before. When was that? Oh my God: embarrassing. *I did a film here.* It was called, I don't know, *Something Somethings Something.* Didn't win any awards. The shoot was totally hot, though. The air conditioning was, like, broken or something. That's why we were so sweaty. Usually they spray it on.

Yeah, I'll have the lobster bisque, and then the lobster stuffed with steak, and do you still have that champagne, the cute one? I'll have a bottle of that, thanks.

Oh, and could I also get a lobster to go? My kitty, Fluffer,

---

[*] J. B. Daniels, contract player for Hot Streaming Angel, of Van Nuys.

loves lobster and if I come home and he smells it on me and I don't have one for him, look out! And better put another bottle of champagne in the bag, too.

Not that hungry, huh? I am starving. I mean, after the day I had today.

You don't mind me talking about work, do you? Today was completely out of control. We had this new sound guy, and at lunch the director's going over all the stuff we did in the morning, and the boom (that's the microphone) is in every shot! In this one shot, it's in *my hair*! So unprofessional! We had to shoot every scene over again! Which sucked, because I always do my best work in the morning. After lunch I'm basically worthless.

Plus it was with Dom. Dom Juan. The "Destroyer"? He wishes. Anyway, I don't like working with him.

Because he's inconsiderate. Those guys always are. I shouldn't be telling you this, it's supposed to be a secret. But Dom is . . . F . . . B . . . I. Everybody knows it. He's part of some big undercover sting operation. You'd think after six years he'd have undercovered something. I mean, what's left to infiltrate? He infiltrated me!

eeHaw eeHaw eeHaw

Anyway, I ended up making an extra $1,300 because they shot something they weren't supposed to.

Just something that wasn't in the contract. If it's not in the contract, and you do it and they shoot it, they have to pay you extra. Although there's some stuff that's not in the contract that I don't do, ever, not even by accident. I've got to protect the J. B. Daniels brand.

Oh, I just picked it. According to the union, your porn star name is supposed to be the name of the pet you had as a kid and then the name of the street you grew up on. But mine, Prince Charles, was already taken and not very indicative of what I do, so I went with J. B. Daniels. It's sort of in honor of my dad.

This is the best champagne.

So, what do you do?

That is *so cool*. I always wanted to be a doctor. I was going to be an anesthesiologist, because I thought it would be nice to *take away* people's pain, you know what I mean? Or I guess I could just be one of those doctors who prescribe pain pills. But that's like eight years of college, and I'd have to get my GED first.

You don't prescribe pain pills, do you?

The weather? You're a weatherman? Then why'd you say you were a doctor? *Oh.* I was wondering where my meteor was.

eeHAW eeHAW eeeeeHAW eeeeehee

No, ma'am, I will *not* quiet down. I am here, having some enjoyable conversation with my date, who paid, like, $8,000, and so if he says something funny, I'm going to laugh, okay? Honestly, I don't give a shit what anniversary you're having.

Oh, look, now she's going to the manager. DON'T FORGET TO TELL HIM HOW YOU'VE BEEN FARTING ALL NIGHT! I mean, talk about affecting the quality of everybody's meal.

I am never going back there again, and you shouldn't either. They completely disrespected you. Listen, you can drop me here. I can't have guys knowing exactly where I live. You understand.

I had a great time, too, the with-you part. And thank you

again; that was so generous of you to bid so much for me. But it's for a good cause. Sick kids, right? I'm doing a PSA for them that's going in the front of all my DVDs.

So I guess this is "good night." But don't think I'm getting out of this car without a hug!

Ooooooooooooooooooooooooh. I love hugs.

They feel real, don't they?

Disengagements

Brynne Scavullo and Sean Martini hooked up at a party two weeks ago. Ms. Scavullo and Mr. Martini hooked up again at a party the following weekend. When they failed to hook up at a party this past Saturday, Ms. Scavullo lamented that it was the end of what could have been a beautiful arrangement.

Alysa Maguire and Dustin Canfield met at a church pancake breakfast on January 9. They agreed to separate earlier this month, based on Ms. Maguire's unwillingness to try specific new things. Mr. Canfield has agreed to find a new congregation, his fifth in the past two years.

Tracy Hanky and Jerome Panke began dating last November based on a shared amusement at the thought of their potential hyphenated surname. In late February, Ms. Hanky extended the riff to include "having a little Hanky-Panke," at which point Mr. Panke felt the joke had played itself out.

Cyndra Pettibone's two-year office flirtation with Stanley Bendix came to an abrupt end last week when Mr. Bendix's cubicle, adjacent to the women's restroom, was moved as part of a legal settlement.

Gwynne Weidner and Ian Buckman met on March 5 at the Hole, a local pub. Mr. Buckman proposed shortly before 1 a.m., and Ms. Weidner accepted. Mr. Buckman rescinded the proposal at approximately 4 a.m., at which point Ms. Weidner allegedly assaulted Mr. Buckman with his five-hundred-dollar Bose clock radio, according to police reports. Charges are pending, but both parties agree the relationship is probably over.

Lara Bernard and Evan Farquar began an online romance in July 2010 after Ms. Bernard purchased a first edition of *The Lost Princess of Oz* on eBay and discovered the beautiful inscription Mr. Farquar had written to a previous girlfriend. A shared interest in the beloved characters of L. Frank Baum blossomed into online fantasy role-playing, with Ms. Bernard as Dorothy and Mr. Farquar as the Scarecrow, the Tin Man, the Cowardly Lion, the Mayor of Munchkin Land, a flying monkey, or any combination thereof; and vice versa. When Ms. Bernard and Mr. Farquar finally met f2f at the Chittenango, New York, Oz-Stravaganza earlier this month, it became apparent there had been dissembling on both sides. Ms. Bernard and Mr. Farquar agreed to fornicate and part.

* * *

Kym Wrona and Douglas Pasternak struck up a conversation February 22 at the Pink Tiger, Ms. Wrona's place of employment. Their budding relationship hit an impasse on March 3 when Ms. Wrona learned that Mr. Pasternak is married and has four children, all under the age of six. Mr. Pasternak is hoping for reconciliation, and has been tipping accordingly.

In October 2010, Sierra Duplaines and Hank Russell "met cute" at an antiabortion rally organized by Mr. Russell outside the Moline Women's Health Co-Op, which is run by Dr. Duplaines. Contrary to their expectations of a screwball romance in the *Adam's Rib* mold, what followed was eleven months of soul-crushing ugliness occasionally relieved by only slightly better-than-average sex. Dr. Duplaines is now reading all the available literature on lesbianism and Mr. Russell is spearheading an effort to pass a constitutional amendment taking away a woman's right to talk.

Ivy Wheeler has declared her torrid six-year affair with Kyle Brindley to be all a figment of Mr. Brindley's fevered imagination. Mr. Brindley responds that Ms. Wheeler is simply angry about his recent fling with the cast of *Glee*.

Paige Mellon and Serge Handler began dating at Ms. Mellon's sister's wedding in August 1999. They dated until February 2007 and again from October 2007 until last month. On February 14 of this year, Ms. Mellon suggested it was time for Mr. Handler "to shit or get off the pot." Mr. Handler responded that if Ms. Mellon thought of herself as a toilet, perhaps she had some personal work to do before being ready for a serious relationship. Mr. Handler is now engaged to some girl right out of high school.

Harley Wozniak and Peter May met in January at Discotyke, where they had brought their children from previous marriages. On March 7, Ms. Wozniak expressed reservations with continuing to see Mr. May, arguing that Mr. May had not left his previous marriage behind. Mr. May argued that yes he had left his previous marriage behind and that it was Ms. Wozniak who had called her ex-husband on her cell phone 112 times in the past month. Ms. Wozniak immediately ended the relationship and demanded that Mr. May hand back her daughter. Ms. Wozniak's girlfriends have since pointed out that Mr. May's theft of her garbage was evidence that he was no longer obsessed with his ex-wife. Ms. Wozniak's and Mr. May's four-year-old daughters have also become close, which is a factor. Ms. Wozniak is unsure what she will do when she sees Mr. May at their daughters' Dirty Dancing class on Saturday.

Lynda Schmeltzer and Geoff Punt began dating in November, ending Ms. Schmeltzer's long string of unhealthy relationships with assholes. Mr. Punt is now an asshole.

Life Without Leann: A Newsletter

By the time you receive this, it will have been more than five hundred days and nearly seventy-five weeks since Leann and I broke up, and, while I cannot proclaim our long ordeal ended, I am pleased to report some encouraging developments in that direction.

LEANN WATCHER OF THE WEEK...

Kudos (and a two-year subscription to LWL) for Warren, of Evanston, Ill., who so eloquently and informatively captures a brief encounter he had with Leann on Nov. 13.

"Leann has lost some weight," Warren writes, "but she is no less beautiful for it. She says she has been exercising, taking classes, doing this, doing that. It appeared to me that she was struggling to fill some void. Your name didn't come up, but it wasn't so much what she said, as what she didn't say."

OUR STRUGGLE CONTINUES . . .

If only it could all be such good news. But unfortunately, OPERATION: TERRIBLE MISTAKE has not been the success we anticipated, and I'm afraid we may have to rethink our strategy.

As you may recall (LWL #57), the operation's objectives were to: (1) apply societal pressure; (2) foster emotional uncertainty; (3) precipitate re-evaluation; and ideally, (4) achieve reconciliation.

The following conversation starter was suggested:

LEANN, I WAS SO SORRY TO HEAR ABOUT YOU AND LARRY. YOU MAKE SUCH A WONDERFUL COUPLE. SO, I DON'T MIND TELLING YOU, I THINK YOU ARE MAKING A TERRIBLE MISTAKE. THIS IS MY OWN PERSONAL OPINION ON THE MATTER.

Unfortunately, a number of well-meaning individuals took this suggestion rather more literally than intended, and repeated it verbatim to Leann, creating a cumulative effect other than the one desired.

I have now received word through an intermediary that Leann requests I "call off the zombies." I will honor her wishes, as always, though I must emphasize I cannot be held responsible for the behavior of individuals acting on their own initiative.

LEANN ANONYMOUS . . .

In our first meeting at Gatsby's, the bartender, Ted, graciously accommodated us by closing off the back room and supplying extra folding chairs. All in attendance praised the wisdom of moving these mutual support sessions from my apartment, which some had complained was not neutral territory, and which had become quite cramped in any case. (On a related matter, Ted told me privately that while he appreciates our patronage, he'd prefer in the future we try not to monopolize the jukebox, or at least play a variety of songs. He says if he doesn't see some improvement the Cowboy Junkies selections will have to go.)

We ordered a round, and at Tom's suggestion, dispensed with the reading of the minutes. We proceeded immediately to old business, continuing debate on Leann's eyes and whether they are a turbulent sea green or a sand-flecked moon blue. It appeared there could be no middle ground on the issue, until Dick stood up and declared, "To paraphrase Elton John, 'Who cares if they're blue or if they're green, those are the sweetest eyes I've ever seen.'"

The motion to adopt Dick's language carried unanimously, and we collected more change for the jukebox.

We ordered another round, and conversation turned naturally to the rest of Leann: her quirky perky nose, her funny sunny smile, the perfect curve of her neck, her soft shoulders, and so on, until petty jealousies precluded further discussion.

Soon thereafter, we took a break to order more refreshments, and then it was time to welcome new members. A stubby and not particularly attractive man, who had been spotted with Leann as recently as mid-October, stood up in the back of the room.

"My name is Harry," he said, "and I love Leann."

Harry then related his long, sad tale, the details of which we are all too familiar, ending with that same old refrain.

"She met this guy," he said. "She says she's deliriously happy."

"Deliriously happy, eh?" Wolfgang said slowly, staring into his beer. "He's *doomed*."

Those of us who could still laugh did so.

"Really?" Harry said, cheering considerably. "So you think there's a chance I can win her back?"

This question precipitated rancorous debate, leading to the inevitable threats of violence and ceasing only when Quentin moved we change the name of our group from Lovers of Leann to Victims of Leann. The motion was soundly defeated, and we voted to adjourn.

Elmo closed the meeting by singing "Oh, Leann," including a new verse that had recently come to him in a dream:

> *Oh, Leann,*
> *I love you,*
> *Love you still,*
> *I love you,*
> *I love you,*
> *I love you still,*
> *I always will.*

LEANN ALERT . . .

My special friend Jane, who has been so supportive during this difficult time, has suggested there is a need for a group addressing the concerns of the lovers of the Lovers of Leann. Anybody who knows somebody who might be interested in such a group should have them write to Leann Anon at this address.

THIS WEEK'S LEANN CHALLENGE . . .

Leann is what she eats, but how well do you know what she eats? Everybody knows Leann likes horseradish on her hamburgers, but how many of you know what *kind* of horseradish? (Here's a hint: She received a case of it last Christmas.)

The answer to last week's challenge: From left to right.

LEANN'S MAILBAG . . .

The mail ran heavy this week with entries to the "Candid Leann" photo contest, and it's obvious I need to remind everyone that the rules clearly stipulate that Leann must be the only person shown in the photograph.

In consideration of those who may wish to resubmit, I've decided to extend the deadline two weeks, until Dec. 10. And remember, entries cannot be returned.

One of our far-flung correspondents, Miles, writes from New Orleans, "I'm going to be in town in the near future, and I was hoping to finally meet this Leann I've heard so much about. Do you have her phone number or an address where I can write her directly?"

No need for that, Miles. Just send your correspondence to Leann in care of this newsletter, and I'll make sure she gets it.

And finally, Reggie, of Oak Lawn, Ill., writes in and asks:

"Larry, isn't it time you got on with your life? It's been nearly two years [*sic*] since Leann broke up with you [*sic*], and I hate to be the one to tell you, pal, but it's over. O-V-E-R [*sic*].

"But listen," Reggie continues, "there are a lot of other chicks in the sea, my friend, and they're yours for the picking. Go for it!"

Well, Reggie, I don't know quite how to answer that. It's difficult to determine exactly what it is you're driving at, since I'm afraid I do not share your bitter perspective, or your particular gift for playground aphorisms. So please understand when I suggest this: You know nothing about love.

But thanks for the letter, Reg. Your "Larry Loves Leann" T-shirt is in the mail.

My Heart: My Rules

If this thing is going to work, and I for one am pulling for it, things are going to have to be different. Not different than they have been for us, certainly, because at the very least I hope we can agree that you and I are not yet an *us* (that being my sincere goal), but different than the way things have been for me, and I suspect have also been for you.

We're not kids anymore, so let's be adults about this. The countless past couplings (and perhaps I am getting ahead of myself here, but I believe they should remain countless) that propel you and me into each other's arms have taught us both, individually, that love, alas, does not conquer all, and that for these things to work, there have to be rules.

My Apartment

As we walk around my apartment, please note:

1. This is my apartment.
2. As the result of years of painstaking trial and error, the television, stereo, thermostat, refrigerator, toaster, and furniture in this apartment are all set at their optimal levels in every regard. Any attempt to adjust any appliance or object in my apartment will only
   a. result in them having to be reset, and
   b. introduce passive-aggressiveness into the relationship, which, as any book on the subject will tell you, is bad.
3. In the closet here, *and this is very important,* are my clothes. No clothes that are not these clothes, or which do not hew very closely to these clothes in matters of style or substance, will ever become my clothes. *They may*
   a. reside in this closet for a while, leading to the impression that they are actively participating in my wardrobe, but
   b. in fact, will be there *for display purposes only;* and
   c. all non-me apparel, regardless of its source, will eventually end up in this closet way over here, where, if you see anything you like, help yourself.
4. I have achieved a satisfying equilibrium between my desire for order and the seductive lure of chaos. Please do not upset it. (See 2.b, above.)
5. I cannot accept responsibility for items of clothing or other personal objects left in the apartment, nor can I vouch for the prov-

enance of any vesture or garniture you discover that proves to be
neither yours nor mine.

6. My lease forbids me from making an extra set of keys.

Me

Generally, there is only one rule about me: I am what I am. But over
the years, a few areas concerning me have cropped up often enough
that I feel the need to address them specifically.

1. I have worn my hair long, short, left, right, straight back, and
   spiked. The particular style you see now is, unfortunately, the
   only one that works. Previous hair experiments by otherwise
   well-meaning individuals have ended in tears.
2. I am ten pounds overweight. When I raise this issue, typically in
   the mornings or just before dessert, you should
   a. be aware that *there is no correct response,* and
   b. quietly go about your business.
3. Do not touch me here, here, and especially *here,* even in jest.
4. I have a medical condition that I may invoke from time to time to
   explain certain moods or behaviors. Do not be alarmed, as this
   condition
   a. is not fatal, in the medical sense;
   b. cannot be transmitted through sexual contact; and
   c. cannot be transmitted through oral sex.

You

Having insisted that I am what I am, it would be hypocritical of
me to not let you be you. However, experience has taught me that you

may, at some point, decide not to be you anymore. Should you antici-pate such a transformation, I ask that you keep in mind:

1. Your hair is perfect. There is no need for you to ever do anything interesting to it.
2. However it is that you smell that way, continue to do so. Sudden shifts in the olfactory landscape disconcert me.
3. If I should come to love you (See Us: 3.a, below), I will of course love you at any size. Yet I cannot love and respect someone who, by all appearances, does not love and respect herself. *Accordingly,*
    a. Do you really want to eat that?
4. All of the above notwithstanding, I do not wish to discourage you from pursuing cosmetic surgery if it would somehow bolster your self-esteem, and would be happy to support you, in a strictly advisory capacity. (Brochures attached.)

Us

Someday very soon (here's hoping!) you and I will be an us. *We will be a much better us, I believe, if we adhere to two simple maxims: we are what we are, and* que será, será. *Regrettably, repeated inqui-ries on particular us-related topics in the past have prompted me to codify this general philosophy into a few, for the want of a better word, edicts.*

1. Even as an us, it is important that you and I remain you and me. This is particularly important with respect to our respective do-miciles (See My Apartment); I suggest, therefore, that you and I endeavor to maintain the roles of *host* and *visitor* in each other's

residence at all times, even while presenting an *us* persona to the
public. In other words,

    a. the host shall be responsible for maintaining an ad-
       equate supply of beverages and snacks in accordance
       with known preferences of the visitor, such beverages
       and snacks to be *offered* and *served* by the host in the
       traditional manner;

    b. in order to prevent a de facto living-together situation,

        i. the visitor shall not stay overnight in the host's res-
           idence more than three (3) days in a row, nor more
           than four (4) days in any one seven-day period, bar-
           ring an emergency at the visitor's residence, includ-
           ing but not limited to: fire, painters, plumbers, an
           especially heinous crime within a two-block area,
           or mice, in which case the maximum stay shall be
           extended to not more than six (6) days;

        ii. combined overnight visits in either residence shall
           not exceed five (5) in any one week, nor fifteen (15)
           in any calendar month; and,

        iii. at the end of an evening in which an overnight stay
           is anticipated, that evening's prospective visitor
           shall not suggest to the prospective host that they
           go "home" nor use a similar locution.

    c. In the event that a misunderstanding, altercation, or
       mood makes an anticipated overnight stay suddenly ill-
       advised,

        i. the visitor, and not the host, will implicitly ac-
           knowledge this fact by announcing, "Well, I've got

        to be going," in a cheerful, non-recriminating man-
ner, while

   ii. at no time will the host question the visitor's moti-
vation for leaving, nor use force to prevent his exit,
or to hasten it.

2. Intimacy will become all but inevitable over time; however,
please note:

   a. it should not be confused with love, and

   b. may involve the release of emotional, historical, or med-
ical information which is private and privileged, and
should not be divulged

     i. to "best" friends over lunch, or

    ii. during family or police interrogations, or

   iii. before gatherings in bars or at parties, even if said
information is presented in a jocular fashion which
"nobody took seriously."

3. Love is a funny, unpredictable thing, and as such follows a time-
table all its own. If past experience is any guide, declarations as
such are meaningless anyway. But the futility of love in a loveless
world notwithstanding,

   a. should I come to love you (keep those fingers crossed),
you will be informed

     i. first in writing, most likely in the closing of a letter
or card, or perhaps on a balloon, and then,

    ii. orally, at some later date,

   iii. both these conditions being necessary to constitute
a lasting and abiding love.

   b. Should you come to love me before I am able to make a
co-declaration of same, you should

      i. exercise restraint in your declarations, as

      ii. more than three (3) unreciprocated declarations of love within a forty-eight-hour period shall be considered harassment.

   c. Any declaration of love shall be considered in effect and at full strength unless and until it is rescinded explicitly.

   d. Any repeated request for a redundant declaration of love, if granted, shall not then be vitiated on the grounds it had to be coerced.

4. Previous loves, as much as we try to leave them behind, will inevitably show up at parties, funerals, and other social occasions. Should this occur, all I ask is

   a. a three-by-five (3 x 5) inch card, spelling out in clear, block letters

      i. his occupation and estimated salary,

      ii. a general description of looks and size,

      iii. the beginning and end dates of the relationship,

      iv. any emotional or physical "firsts,"

      v. reason for dissolution, and

      vi. whether you ever really loved him,

   b. such information provided with sufficient time for me to recuse myself from the proceedings with cause, and without causing a scene.

   c. Likewise, and happily, I will supply you with comparable information, should you request it in writing, and provided, in my sole estimation, you can handle it.

5. I have been hurt; you have been hurt. I do not wish to hurt you. I trust you do not want to hurt me. None of this should be forgotten should any future hurt occur.

Sunday Mornings

I propose the following schedule and general guidelines:

9:00 a.m.   Awake, snooze, spoon.
9:15–10:30   Breakfast.
    a. Coffee.
        i. Half-and-half should be available; low-fat or skim will be considered a violation of the spirit of Me: 2.b. No flavored blends, please.
    b. Bagels (host fetches), cream cheese, butter, etc.
    c. Fruit (in season).
9:30–12:30 p.m.   Sunday New York Times.
    a. In five piles: Unread, You've Read, I've Read, Both Read, Coupons.
    b. No reading aloud.
    c. Host commandeers the crossword but
        i. makes an attempt to include the visitor in the crosswording process, even if she can do all of it herself.
        ii. No dictionaries.
12:30   Sex, showering, as mood permits.

Miscellaneous

From my experience in previous situations, I have learned a few things which, God willing, can prevent any future us from becoming the emotional baggage that burdens any subsequent us you or I may pursue separately.

1. Preexisting cat(s; up to two) will be tolerated, provided you do not insist they become an active third party in the relationship. Should you not now have such a cat, but consider acquiring one in the future, I would appreciate:
   a. the right to peremptorily challenge up to three prospective names; and
   b. verbal assurances that said creature will be nurtured from a pool of affection and attention created especially for it, and not from other sources.

2. Absolutely no dog sharing.

3. My medication does not interact with alcohol, and while we're on the subject,
   a. I only drink to forget those aspects of my past that might otherwise impede our ability to form a lasting, loving *us*.
   b. I know my limit.

4. From time to time I may disappear for several days, physically and/or emotionally.
   a. This need not concern you.
   b. Under no circumstance call the police.

5. If your name is Katherine, Kathy, Kate, Cate, Kat, Kay, Sweetie, or Punkin, it might be wise for me to call you by your middle name, or a third, mutually agreed upon moniker. One possibility: Nancy.

6. One night four to six months from now, we may go out to eat, see a movie, come back to my apartment, make love, watch some TV, go to bed, and you will awake in the middle of the night to find me weeping.

    a.   It will be nothing.

    b.   Ignore it and go back to sleep.

7.   Please refrain from talking during sex.

Before you say anything: don't say anything. I know what you're going to say, and I agree: it would be so nice if we were young and unbruised again and could rush in like fools where, as adults, we know better than to tread. This is not to say I am not all for this. I just think that if you and I must dance once again into that dark, warm room filled with spiders, we ought to step carefully; and I want to know ahead of time that no more than a handful is playing violins behind their backs.

Oh, and one more thing: I don't dance.

Ask the Eight Ball

Will Marissa and I ever get back together?

REPLY HAZY
TRY
AGAIN

Will Marissa and I ever get back together?

MY REPLY
IS
NO

Will Marissa and I ever get back together?

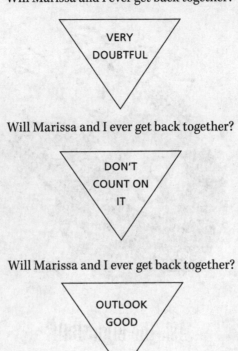

Will Marissa and I ever get back together?

Will Marissa and I ever get back together?

Glee

I will do a book.

—Karl Rove

Portrait in Evil: My Story

It's not easy being the bad guy. The public hates you, and no wonder, fed as they are a steaming stream of media bile that maliciously misrepresents all your plots and machinations. Adults, in turn, poison the minds of the young, who every day joyously play-act your murder. All you have are your minions, who do your bidding, sure, but out of fear and not out of respect or, dare I say it, love.

Little do people realize that under the mask, beneath the armor, lie the beating hearts, the transmogrified flesh and isotopic blood of a creature who was once very much human, just like them. If they were to take a moment to peer through that translucent skull and into that superevolved brain they would find more than dark schemes and deadly schemata and vast enemies lists; they would discover, deep inside, tucked behind some new torture notions, the tiny, sad boy with the freakishly large head who only wanted to be good but was turned bad.

This is the story I wish to tell. The story of the Dr. Cranius I know. *My* story.

I will begin with my origin story, not the ridiculous tale told in comic books and by Nancy Grace without regard to libel laws but the true telling of my humble, tragic beginnings: my miraculous birth to a poor, single dry-cleaner who lost her pelvis as a result of the delivery and was therefore ruined for other men, dooming me to be raised without a proper male role model. Very little is written about my sainted mother other than that I eventually killed her; nothing is known of the love that shone through her revulsion, or her heroic struggles to pay for all the appliances her precocious toddler dismantled, or the punitively expensive custom protective headgear. This is the woman I want people to know. Perhaps then they will understand why she had to die.

The hard child is mother to the man, the poet wrote, and I was a very hard child. Hardened, by the playground taunts of Big Head, Giant Head, Huge Head, Humungous Head, and, eventually, Colossal Head. Hardened, by an educational system unable to distinguish genius from madness, and forced to ride the little yellow bus with the drool patrol. Hardened, every day at school, a diamond in a coal mine, my brilliance blinding eyes unaccustomed to the light, destroying principals unwilling to cede power to their superior.

I dropped out.

It was never my intention to turn evil. At first, I was simply trying to survive—hawking my scientific papers on the streets of Urbana, performing calculus tricks down by the boardwalk, busking π to the centillionth on the subway. I often went hungry.

And so there was a certain situational or perhaps cosmic irony in the fact that it was my determination to use my prodigious gifts for the greater good that led to my current profession. Frustrated by the many cretins and tomfools I encountered in my daily life, I devoted myself to elevating the public to a level worthy of discourse. The result was Dr. Cranius's Brain Liquid, a mental-energy drink that combined the best of ancient oriental botanicals with a secret boost of radiographically induced evolution. I brought the product to PepsiCo in late 1993, and they rejected it after merely tasting it. Of course, less than eighteen months later these fiends announced Josta, a pale imitation of my drink without any of its mutagenic qualities.

Even then, I resisted the lure of villainy. Rather than contaminate this interloper with retarding agents, which would have been very easily done, I redoubled my efforts to beat them to market, which resulted in the drink lab accident that made me the Dr. Cranius I am today: stronger, smarter, albeit a little insane, and, yes, evil.

The middle section of the book will concentrate on what it is like to be the reigning supervillian of Urbana, going behind the headlines and news bulletins to reveal my day-to-day struggles. I can't go out to a restaurant without a legion of half-assed heroes crashing my table before the salad even arrives. I run through minions faster than I can replace them. I can't get a cab, going uptown or downtown.

I will also lay out my plans for global domination, and I

think readers will be surprised how reasonable and pleasant a Dr. Cranius reign would be. I believe this section will guarantee me a spot on the all-important Jon Stewart show, or failing that, *The Colbert Report*.

On the advice of my agent, I will also not stint on "the dirt." While I cannot reveal the details here, I have information about Red Hawk and his young ward, Chick, that is certain to make the tabloids. As for myself, it is eternally true that a certain kind of woman is attracted to a bad man, and I have had more than my share. I will provide a list of names, and why they had to die. I also have a very funny story about Jen Aniston.

Bidding starts at *one billion dollars*.

Recent Advances in Interpersonal Grooming, If I Had My Way

Magic Wart Wand

A personal laser that removes unsightly blemishes from people sitting across from you on the train or bus without them knowing it.

The Sniffer

An electronic device that can identify unpleasant smells as well as the person emitting them.

Man Up!

Sonic pulse generator that causes onlookers to see you as more handsome and better groomed than you really are by inducing a series of microstrokes in your date, job interviewer, etc.

Personal Space Saver

A handheld microwave gun that reduces the Body Mass Index of the obese person spilling over the armrest of your theater or airline seat by liquefying adipose tissue into a yellowish oil which is then excreted through the nearest available orifice.

Germoshield

A 360-degree irradiator that destroys all bacteria and viruses, along with the organisms carrying them, within an eighteen-foot circle of cleanliness.

A scientist has set off an international furor by suggesting that it might soon be feasible to transplant ovaries from aborted fetuses into infertile women who do not make viable eggs of their own. Dr. Roger Gosden, a researcher at Edinburgh University, said . . . he already has accomplished this in mice.

"If you take a more adventuresome and experimentalist approach . . . you have a chance to see if it does more harm than good," said Dr. John Fletcher, an ethicist at the University of Virginia.

—*New York Times*

Adventures in Experimentation

Much of what I know about human anatomy I owe to Brenda King, and, before her, to Leonardo da Vinci. It was Brenda who, in the eighth grade, allowed me to run my finger along the entire length of her appendectomy scar, and it was da Vinci whose sixteenth-century dissections of corpses at the hospital of Santa Maria Nuova in Florence laid the groundwork for modern science's triumphant experimental subject: the Visible Man.

The Visible Man, with its transparent "skin," durable hand-painted organs, and raw-pink plastic guts, taught me more about physiology than four years at any stupid medical school would have. Many were the happy hours I hunkered down in my bedroom laboratory, rapturously disassembling my Visible Men and putting them back together again, remaking them into startling new bioconfigurations: the four-armed dual-cardiac Visible Man with double pumping action; the all-liver-and-kidneys Visible Man, theoretically capable of drinking his weight every forty minutes; the gutless Visible Man with secret storage compartment for steelies, clearies, and cat's-eyes. Who knows what I might have accomplished if Pete Maguire's brother hadn't gotten a whole mess of M-80s on a trip to Indiana that summer?

Just as my parents and teachers were shocked and frightened by my notebook sketches, so too were da Vinci's contemporaries disturbed by his dismantling of dead Florentines. He was called a ghoul by citizens without the foresight to see the rewards that his anatomical studies would reap—not just Visible Man but the Operation and Twister board games, and let's not forget Visible Woman. As a freelance experimentalist, I must persevere, then, despite rejection from the medical establishment and the lack of federal funding; I must publish my work, wherever I can, in hopes of generating badly needed funds for some fresh tools.

EXPERIMENT 107: Grafting the hands of a capuchin monkey onto a Labrador retriever, I created a dog that can not only throw a tennis ball sixty yards while playing fetch with itself, but also scratch the back of its master, a task that many dogs long to do but, sadly, cannot. (Originally published in *Puppy Master,* April 2007.)

EXPERIMENT 113B: Using a gene-splicing technique found online somewhere, I incorporated genetic material from a Dow Scrubbing Bubble into a purr-free feline zygote, producing a Siamese cat with a less neurotic disposition and claws that extrude rug-and-furniture shampoo. (*Industrial Pet,* Winter 2008.)

EXPERIMENT 235F: By sewing live white mice directly onto the heads of male American bald eagles, I hoped to cosmetically augment their thinning pates and thus increase the breeding success of this species. Unfortunately, the subjects were brutally attacked by their mates—out of jealousy, I hypothesize. (*Annals of Mice,* March 2010.)

EXPERIMENT 482: Just last Friday, I xenotransplanted 150 hummingbird hearts into a sixty-eight-year-old man suffering from congestive heart failure. I theorized that if the man's body rejected one or even several of the hearts there would still be dozens left to do the job. However, the operation proved more complicated than anticipated, taking nearly an hour and necessitating a drugstore mobilization for more thread. As the last stitch was put in place, the man jumped off the kitchen table, ran one hundred meters in

8.64 seconds, and expired. Based on these results, I have decided to use artichoke hearts next time. (*Bird Fancy,* under review.)

I am currently seeking volunteers for two experiments: 486—"Transgrafting Eyebrows to Outer Ear in Human Subject"; and 487—"Box Turtles Surgically Installed in Human Large Intestine." In the former case, the goal is to create natural, renewable earmuffs; in the latter, the hope is it will make a nice home for the turtles.

I Killed Them in New Haven

How you all doing tonight? It's great to be here at the Loco Lobo, assuming this is Tuesday. You know, it just so happens, I'm a little loco. Kinda crazy, zany guy. You're looking at one kooky dude. Wacky, nutty, unbalanced, disturbed, incompetent to stand trial: I've been called all those things.

Anyone here from Chicago? I'm from Chicago. You, sir: you're from Chicago? You're not me, are you?

Hahahahahahahahahahahahahahahahahahahahaha.

I have a lot of weird thoughts. You ever wonder why, for example, seven times eight is fifty-six? What *genius* decided that one? I don't remember voting. Or where socks go when they disappear from dryers? Is it the Pentagon? I think you know it is.

Anybody else here watch TV? Me, I watch a lot of TV. A lot of TV. Because, you know, when you're not watching it, it can watch you. So I watch TV pretty much all the time. Have you seen this *Gilligan's Island*? Seven stranded castaways on a desert-island paradise? What is *up* with *that*? All I know is if I was Gilligan and it was my island, I'd sure as shit be fucking that Ginger. Am I right? And Mary Ann. And the rest. I'd be lying naked in my hammock with those two gals and Mrs. Howell and the Professor, and drinking sweet, sweet coconut juice out of the Skipper's skull. Am I right?

Hey, remember that lady who'd fallen and couldn't get up? *I've fallen and I can't get up. I've fallen and I can't get up.* You know why she can't get up, don't you? Because they control the gravity and she found out.

You can bet I'd be having sex with her, too.

Travel a lot in this job. Gotta keep moving, or you get pulled into the earth by the trolls. What is *their* problem?

So I fly a lot, on planes mostly. Airline food: now, what demented individual came up with this item? I mean, who eats chicken? What if the chickens found out? They would not be happy.

Can't get a decent knife on an airplane anymore. It's all plastic now. Like, what? I'm going to stab and stab and stab the passenger sitting next to me? And how do they know what you're thinking? Here's a hint: don't eat the peanuts.

They've got a lot of crazy laws in this country. Screwy

laws. Like in Tennessee, it's illegal to stand in the middle of the street, *even if you've been instructed by the highest authority to do so*. And in Maine it's against the law to spit on babies. Pretty babies, ugly babies, it doesn't matter. Crazy. They'll arrest you for anything.

Am I the only one here planning on shooting the president? Show of hands: Who's with me?

That's right, best keep it to yourself. They can trace your e-mails now, using DNA that the keys on the keyboard extract from your fingertips. I can't believe I invented that technology and then they go and use it against me. Totally nuts.

Hey, you know what I hate? Don't you hate it when people laugh at you? Like *you're all laughing at me right now*.

I'm going to cry for a little bit. Could we turn off the mike and take the lights down?

Great. I'm done!

How are those margaritas treating you? Strange name, margarita. Means "little Margaret." The funny thing is, she tastes nothing like that. It's just insane. Can I have a sip of yours? Thanks. Delicious. I hope you don't mind; I have every kind of cancer. Including a couple of new ones the NIH just disseminated.

I'm a little neurotic when it comes to food. I won't eat anything orange. The color doesn't actually exist, which should be a tip-off. I also won't eat possum, because you can never tell if it's really dead. And when I kill and eat my enemies, who are legion, I forgo the eyeballs, because I don't want them checking out my insides and reporting back to *you know who*.

Well, that flashing light means that either Jesus has come for me as promised or my time is up. So I'd just like to leave you with this thought:

Good night! And don't forget to tip your waitresses, especially that one over there: she's in love with me.

Are You Insane?

Take this simple quiz to find out if you are insane.

1. If someone bumped into me on the street, I would:
   a. Say "Excuse me" and continue walking.
   b. Say "Excuse me" but sarcastically, and continue walking.
   c. Not say "Excuse me" and stand there giving the person a dirty look as he or she continued walking.
   d. Other: _____

How You Did: If you answered a, b, or c, you are probably not insane, although the sensitivity of this test is limited and you should periodically ask your friends if they think you've been acting crazy lately. If you answered "Other," show your written response to a person picked at random on the street. If s/he runs away from you, you may be insane. Please consult a therapist.

High Spirits

Media Culpa

Apology to Our Readers from Vigilante-Statesman *editor and publisher Bud Hamsterman*

Yesterday, some editions of the *Vigilante-Statesman* contained an editorial criticizing Mayor Bob McNaught for his recent handling of the Crick Creek bond issue. For the record, the Honorable Mayor McNaught, despite his miniature, squatty appearance and frequently affected demeanor, cannot be accurately described as a "mincing dwarf."

True dwarfs, while of somewhat smaller stature than the average person, are otherwise normal, functioning human beings who make valuable contributions to our society. The same certainly cannot be said of Mayor McNaught. In any case, the correct appellation for such size-challenged individuals is "little person."

This has been official *Vigilante-Statesman* style since 2008. Furthermore, it is not this paper's policy to insinuate that dwarfs mince, nor that mincing individuals are dwarfs.

Also, as *Vigilante-Statesman* readers are well aware, this state is considering riverboat gambling as a way to raise much-needed revenue for its education and drug-rehabilitation programs. Thus, depicting Mayor McNaught as "One-Eyed Bob," a nineteenth-century dandy slick replete with a pencil-thin mustache and silk pinstripes, is not simply a bad cliché; it comes at the worst possible time. Moreover, this characterization of the mayor as a dishonest riverboat rogue only perpetuates an ancient stereotype that professional gamblers have worked hard to dispel. To our knowledge, at no time has any professional gambler in this community been linked to the mayor or his activities.

As the newspaper of record in this community, accuracy is our watchword. Nevertheless, a reading of yesterday's editorial suggests that some members of our editorial board were passing notes and not paying attention during Mrs. Anclade's history classes. Specifically, the statement "Like a tiny Napoleon, the mayor stands before those who would improve our school-lunch program and declares, 'Let them eat snack cakes!'" completely disregards the fact that the original quote upon which this misguided attempt at humor is based has never been attributed to Napoleon at all, but rather to some other French person, who most scholars now agree never said it in the first place. Also, while most will acknowledge that Mussolini's foreign policy and human-rights records were poor, to call the mayor a "municipal Mussolini" only reveals our editorial writers' ignorance of the Fascist dictator's successful public-works programs.

And matters of accuracy aside, our editorial board displayed the height of insensitivity by evoking Genghis Khan in this context at a time when his own people are reevaluating the historical importance of this great warrior and, yes, statesman. To our Mongol readers, we apologize.

Our editorial writers had no evidence upon which to claim, even facetiously, that the mayor is the Antichrist. For the record, Bob McNaught is not the Antichrist. The Antichrist is Bryan Reed, Paul Bodeen, and The Ax, three talented musicians who play Thursdays and Fridays at the Goat's Head Soup Kitchen out on Old Schwermer Road. The *Vigilante-Statesman* did not mean to inadvertently imply that these earnest young men were in any way responsible for the slow, inexorable degradation of our fair city into filth and decay.

And finally, we would like to state most emphatically that pigs are actually intelligent and clean animals, and likely would not lie down with the mayor, or any other corrupt official. They are also safe to eat. In an attempt to draw a comparison with the mayor, the editorial failed to make this distinction clear.

We understand the County Farmers' Association is considering canceling "Pork Barrel Days" as a result of this ill-considered metaphor. We hope this will not be the case, and that we can all put this whole unfortunate affair behind us.

Toward that end, I have taken steps as publisher to ensure that the *Vigilante-Statesman* remains free of such offenses in the future. Reluctantly, I have accepted the resignation of Jim Hamsterman, our editorial-page editor, and have suspended without pay our two editorial writers, Ted Nuggles and Lissa McNaught. Lucy Hamsterman, the editorial-page copy editor who should have caught these mistakes, has been reassigned and will not be eligible for this year's World Series tickets pool.

And yet, even this is not enough. In a very real sense, all of us here at the *Vigilante-Statesman* are responsible for fostering the ignorance, prejudice, and unprofessionalism that led to these truly regrettable errors. Therefore, I am announcing that, with this afternoon's sports final, the *Vigilante-Statesman* will cease publication for the next three weeks, during which time I want the remaining staff of this paper to think about what we've done.

CLARIFICATION

In an editorial in yesterday's paper, Mayor Bob McNaught was referred to as Mayor Boob, Mayor McNutt, Boob McNothing, Boo McMuffin, and in a number of other ways that cannot be printed in a family newspaper. According to *Vigilante-Statesman* style, these are all nicknames and should have been identified as such with the use of quotation marks. The *Vigilante-Statesman* regrets the error.

Local Wag

Reprinted with permission from the Manhattan Blue Streak, *the alternative weekly newspaper of Manhattan, Illinois, located just thirteen miles west of Monee. The* Wag *is written by Laurence Doyle, also the paper's editor, publisher, and circulation manager.*

Men are but children of a larger growth.

—Dryden

Pinch Me: That's what our own bachelor mayor squealed repeatedly during his oh-so-surprising *né day soirée* out at the Red Heifer Beefbarn last Friday eve. A consuming politician, **Mayor Ed** moved and shaked from table to table, requesting his Big 55 B-day spankings from Manhattan's more-than-happy-to-oblige business and civic leaders, including longtime Ednemesis **P. Greg Roberts,** who lost count and had to start over—three times.

Mayor Ed was beat red by the time he paddled over to the cheap seats, where the *Times-Caveat*'s **Ron Peterson,** citing his journalistic credentials as a *real* reporter from Manhattan's *real* weekly, refused to "become part of the story." **Wag** didn't mind one bit, though, and when our top public servant further requested "a pinch to grow an inch," we promptly complied—and Wag'll be damned if His Honor didn't grow an inch, at *least . . .*

In town just for the B-bash: the mayor's former college bunk-mate and longtime companion, **John Travolta.** The up-again-down-again-up-again-down-again-up-again actor made a point of letting everyone know how much he loved banging his female wife, who couldn't make it. His Honor the B-day Boy appeared a tiny tad put out by this hetero-than-thou display, but hey, it's his party, he can poop if he wants to . . .

Later, in a private gathering closed to the media, His Pouti-ness bachelorpartied until nearly 1:00 a.m., male celebonding with Travolta, former Indiana **sen. Larry Craig,** and **the Scissor Sisters.**

Still Dying: Perky **Siobhan Mitchell** rallied out of her coma once again last week to make yet another bizarre last wish: to kiss the hand of billionaire songbird **Justin Bieber.** Don't get **Wag** wrong—we'd love to lick the lad's delicate digits ourselves— but what made frisky little Siobhan's wish curious was that she last emerged from consciousness back in *December 2006,* before Bieber's very first YouTube assault. *It's a miracle,* or something.

Well, no sooner than you could say "Front-page banner in the Manhattan *Times-Caveat,*" Master Bieber's private jetcopter was touching down in **Scott Johnson**'s soybeans about 150 yards from Manhattan's own **Ronald McDonald** House. Master Bieber and his *enfantourage* sprinted to the feisty tyke's side only to find they were too late—former childcrooner **Justin Timberlake** had beaten them to the photo op, and the weekly *T-C* had long gone to bed itself, not to mention plucky Siobhan, who had slipped back into her accustomed twilight . . .

Doctor My Thighs: Old Doc Thatcher's practice sure has picked up since he got certified by the Board of Plastic and Reconstructive Surgeons. Recent visitors, according to the doc's poorly guarded records: **Amy Roberts,** who, after giving birth to four of **P. Greg**'s melonheaded offspring, decided it was time to put a little creative tension back into the marriage; middle-aged **Paris Hilton,** who, while in town to sleep with someone in the 60950 zip code, had the bags under her eyes removed and put into quick turnaround as nu-boobs; and **Emilio Estevez,** who hopes that with a few minor alterations he'll be able to find work as a **Charlie Sheen** impersonator.

Self-Wagellation: Just last month, **Wag** predicted that a certain music teacher's frequent duets (and, in one case, a quartet) with members of the pop/rock/metal/reggae/rap/emo/new age/folk contingent would prompt the federal **Centers for Disease Control** to open a branch office here. Well, the recent **Ke$ha** tour clinched it. "This is a situation that bears watching," says **Dr. Sanford Mickle,** the epidemiologist assigned to head up the new office, "particularly with school starting up soon." The CDC outlet will mean five new jobs for the area . . .

Wagola: Due to the recent transfer of all new **Chevy Volt** production to Manhattan's "sister plant" in Puerto Negro, Mexico, **UAW**

Local 289 will be holding its annual Labor Day parade at **Jessy's Budweiser Sign and Dance.**

Waggings: Ben Finestein, Manhattan's own **Jew,** denies rumors that his deli, or Jewish-style restaurant, serves **moth balls.** He says they're called **matzoh balls** (pronounced "Mott's-O," like the applesauce) and are harmless boiled balls of dough. Jews consider them a delicacy, Ben says . . . Those rumors about **Nancy Grace** moving to Manhattan are totally unfounded. The **Wag** hears they were started by an unscrupulous real estate agent hoping to incite panic sales . . . And that wasn't **Erma Bombeck** spotted signing books at **Kym's Kards and Gyfts, Etc.** last Saturday. She's dead. It was **Michael Moore.** Kym apologizes for any misunderstanding . . .

The Last Wag: What pop-ular adult website (and Exhibit T&A in a current court case) features hot young up'n'cummer **Roni Lynn Lords,** who bears an uncanny resemblance to Manhattan's own 2009 Dog Queen, **Pegi Peterson**—or, as she is known around the Peterson Playhouse, **Princess Sweetpea?**

JAILED ACTIVIST 'VISITS' PETS

Fran Stephanie Trutt, convicted of trying to bomb the president of a Connecticut surgical equipment company, said yesterday that she has visited her dogs four times since April as part of the previously undisclosed terms of her plea-bargain.

"I've seen my little ones, and that's the only reason why I took the plea-bargain," Trutt said during a telephone interview from the Niantic State Prison for women.

—As far as you probably got

The Rest of the Story

Trutt is just one of millions of American felons participating in experimental criminal justice programs across the country designed to explore innovative ways of combating alarming increases in criminal activity, which in some cities, such as Detroit, now exceeds the amount of noncriminal activity.

"Despite the fact that state and federal law-enforcement agencies have been very good at getting out the message that certain behaviors are illegal and that people who engage in those behaviors will be punished if caught and convicted, we're still seeing a lot of illegal behavior out there," said Peter Pratt, professor of penology at Michigan State University and editor of the *American Journal of Criminal Justice Theory and Practice.*

"Clearly," Pratt said, "something more needs to be done."

Something more is being done. According to *Crime and Corrections,* a national newsletter advocating noncruel but unusual punishments, novel ways of dealing with lawbreakers are multiplying nearly as fast as the prison populations themselves. Kevin Dradd, editor of *Crime and Corrections,* estimates that the average convicted felon today "would have to get twenty-five years to life just to be able to take advantage of all the programs available to him."

"But this is good," hastened to add Dradd, who has no official affiliation with any academic or law-enforcement agency but describes himself simply as a "penal buff."

"What's *really* cruel is punishment as usual," Dradd quipped. "They say you can catch more flies with honey than with vinegar. Well, the same goes for inmates, except, of course, they're already caught. Perhaps a better way of saying this is that an unhappy, bored criminal is a recidivist criminal."

Variety, and not boredom, is indeed the spice of prison life today. At the Joliet State Penitentiary Petting Zoo just southwest of Chicago, inmates convicted of violent crimes are encouraged to touch and form emotional bonds with dogs, cats, and other small mammals provided by the local anti-cruelty society. On a recent afternoon in the Petting Yard, one burly resident, weighing three hundred pounds and covered with sexually explicit tattoos, spent nearly forty-five minutes gently stroking a large brown-and-taupe Angora rabbit that seemed to almost disappear into the hollow of his cupped hand.

"He's soft," said Jacob Jason Blazz, serving seven consecutive life terms for chopping up a downstate family of four into cubes approximately two inches long on each side, and then attempting to conceal the crime by reassembling the pieces into an entirely different family of five.

"The zoo is very popular with our long-term residents," said Pam Glipp, a spokesperson for the correctional center. "We believe it is helping them to develop an appreciation for the sanctity of life. The hope, of course, is that this will extrapolate out to non-pet animals—humans in particular."

In many cases, it is not inspiration but necessity that has become the mother of inventive penal reform. In Broward County, Florida, which recently saw a 160 percent increase in the number of activities defined as illegal, prison officials have been forced to adopt a "Weekends Off" policy for long-term inmates in order to accommodate the massive influx of white-collar criminals and artists serving weekend sentences.

One state official, whose name was not known at press time, called the program an unprintable expletive.

However, another source close to the program, in an anonymous telephone interview, said of the new "Weekends Off" policy, "We're receiving a lot of complaints from our regulars that they come back Sunday night only to find their cells a mess and valuables missing."

Nevertheless, the overwhelming majority of pioneering correctional tactics has been welcomed as at least worth a try. Many actually have been worth that try.

For example, Massachusetts has abandoned its traditional weekend furlough program in favor of a buddy system; early indications are that crime by prison buddies on furlough will be 25 percent less than both individuals would have been expected to commit separately. Intrabuddy violence is a problem but not a concern, officials there say.

And in Baltimore, the district attorney's office stopped prosecuting cases altogether when it was determined that accused lawbreakers were seven times more likely to commit repeat offenses while out on bail than if they were simply set free.

"When they're bailed out, they feel like they're on somebody else's time" was one explanation offered off the record.

The new policy seems to be working; for the first time in many years, crime in the city is rising only arithmetically.

Perhaps no program has been more successful at reducing crime than the highly successful crime-reducing program launched in Madison, Wisconsin, one of the few remaining bastions of progressive thought in the Midwest, and home of the University of Wisconsin Badgers. The Madison Program, as it is called, is based on the principle that "you should punish the crime and not the criminal," according to Susan Grunn, a local resident.

"Our philosophy is that rules are made to be broken," Grunn said the other day.

Since Madison rescinded its entire penal code in April, effectively making nothing illegal, the city's official crime rate has dropped to zero.

"Obviously," Grunn added.

Freelance File

News item: Stock market in toilet; foreclosures at all-time high; "worse than Great Depression."

CANNED FOODIES *Top chef recipes for gourmet meals using Campbell's Soup, Spaghetti-O's, etc.*

BABY, IT'S HOT INSIDE! *Free heat alternatives. Household objects, furniture rated for combustibility, toxicity.*

THE OTHER MEATS
Should move on these before things improve.

Celebrity Profile Subjects

Miranda Cosgrove (LITTLE BIG GIRL)

Scarlett Johansson (BIG LITTLE GIRL)

Zooey *and* Emily Deschanel (THE NEW BARRYMORES)

Thomas Pynchon (HANGIN' WITH TOM)

News item: Baby boomers getting older.

MACULAR D-D-D-D- GENERATION *As Boomers age, many are faced with difficult choice: laser surgery or glasses? Pros/Cons, personal stories of triumph/tragedy.*

NO REMOTES: STORIES TO TELL TODAY'S GRANDCHILDREN

<u>Service Pieces</u>

9 SEX TRICKS THAT WILL MAKE HIM THINK YOU'VE BECOME A HOOKER *Interview hookers, or just make them up? Test on wife first.*

WHERE TO FIND BEST PORN ON THE WEB *Pseudonym?*

News item: People hate Muslims

SHIITE LIKE ME *Undercover investigative piece. Apply for jobs in turban, etc., at downtown electronics stores. Maybe follow Islam for whole year and make it a book? Strategize on how to get beaten but not killed.*

<u>Travel Pieces</u>

TOP SPAS OF OLD EUROPE

CASTLE KEPT: KING FOR A MONTH

BEST SEX VACATIONS OF SOUTHEAST ASIA

Get passport.

News item: Celebutantes Getting in Trouble

Need new angle. Paradigm shift. Celebutantes as Christians and Paparazzi as Lions?

Possible "Lives" Columns

MILLION LITTLE PIXELS *Reveal Internet porn addiction. Title too clever? Alt:* I NEED PORN *This may be a book.* THE MONSTER IN MY iPAD? *Tell wife now, or wait?*

THROUGH GLASSES DARKLY *On getting reading glasses for first time. Intimations of mortality, etc. Maybe end on reading bedtime story to son or daughter. Circle unbroken. Tearing up already. Ask wife what books they like.*

MY DAD *Dredge something up.*

News item: Dog dials 911

GOOD DOG! *Listicle. Not all dogs dialing phones. Dogs barking at danger, raising babies, etc. Include police, assistance dogs, and this could be book. Literary nonfiction or coffee table? Why not both?*

Or go counterintuitive: THE BEAST IN THE HOUSE, *dogs who killed/maimed/ate owners, in funny way.*

Or humorous twist: CAT HEROES. *Made-up, obviously. Could be "Shouts and Murmurs," or short, funny book.*

Something About Robots

Stop Me If You've Heard This One[1]

Larry Doyle is a professional dinner speaker. The following piece is adapted from opening remarks to a speech he recently gave before the Optimists Club of Manhattan.

New York City is totally insane.[2] Just the other day, I was having a drink at Mulligan's Brew[3] over on Forty-Third Street, when who,

---

1. I would like to most gratefully acknowledge Vince Offer, the independent filmmaker who sued big Hollywood filmmakers Peter and Bobby Farrelly, accusing them of stealing jokes from his film *The Underground Comedy Movie* for their film *There's Something About Mary*. His lawsuit provided important inspiration for this article.
2. Credit must go to professional jokester Sammy Haggis, whose comedic monologue contains this opening sentence, albeit in a slightly different form.
3. Although at the time of its creation, this tavern name was fully a work of

or should I say *what,* should walk into the bar but this pink-and-purple kangaroo.[4]

I'm thinking, Whooooa, bartender, another round, and this time make it a double.[5]

So this 'roo sidles up to the bar, puts a twenty-dollar bill on the counter, and says, "Barkeep, give me a Screaming Orgasm."[6,7]

Hiiiiiii-Yo![8] The bartender is a bit taken aback by this, but he's seen a lot of strange things, so he makes the Screaming Orgasm and plops it down on the bar.

---

the imagination, it has since been pointed out that other drinking establishments with this name actually exist in Boston, Milwaukee, Chicago, and Champaign-Urbana, Illinois.

4. See "What the Who Is at the Zoo?" in *Puppy Dog Tales,* fall 1964, "Wag Bag" page, submitted by Michael Schrage, age seven.

5. Again: Haggis.

6. Credit for creating and naming this specialty drink has been variously attributed to Sebastian Dangerfield, a mixologist at the J.P. Ginger's in Manhattan, and to Flo Wechek, owner of Babylon's Hanging Beer Garden in Fort Repose, Florida.[i]

7. The aforementioned setup, accompanied by the retort "Straight up or on the rocks?" originally appeared in the shooting script of a 1988 *Cheers* episode[ii] but was excised by NBC censors.

8. *See* Ed McMahon, *The Tonight Show,* and his various fully protected lampooners.

---

i The bartenders and drinking establishments in this note are literary allusions to J. P. Donleavy's *The Ginger Man* and Pat Frank's *Alas, Babylon,* respectively.

ii Although the joke may have itself been appropriated in whole or in part from *Shticks and Grins,* a 1979 revue performed by the Hasty Pudding Club of Harvard University.

"How much do I owe you?"[9] asks the kangaroo.

Well, the bartender looks at the double sawbuck[10] on the counter and figures, *This is a kangaroo, what does he know about drink prices?* So he says, "Twenty bucks."

The kangaroo doesn't say anything. He just slams down the drink and hops off his stool to leave.

At this point the bartender's curiosity gets the best of him.[11] He says to the kangaroo, "You know, we've never had a talking pink-and-purple kangaroo in here before."

"Well," the kangaroo says, "at twenty bucks for one lousy Screaming Orgasm, I'm not a bit surprised."[12]

---

9. While historically attributed to the old Jack Benny radio show, this phrase has American literary antecedents which include, but are not limited to, the works of Nathaniel West, Ambrose Bierce, and, of course, Mark Twain. In any event, this particular wording has since become part of the vernacular and can hardly be considered to be the intellectual property of any one author.

10. According to Robert L. Chapman's *New American Dictionary of American Slang,* this term has been employed by Westbrook Pegler, the racist anti-Semite admired by Sarah Palin, among others.

11. This transitory sentence originally appeared in a different context in "The Annoying Foot-High Companion," from *A Thousand Men Walk into a Thousand Bars,* edited by Isaac Asimov.

12. As anyone who reads the papers or watches Fox News must know by now, I have been accused by one "Jerry Grinn" of appropriating this entire humoresque from his book *Grinn's Big Comedy Treasury of Toasts, Roasts, Boasts, and Jests.* I do not take these charges lightly. As a professional writer who derives a not inconsiderable portion of his income from his unique comic sensibility, I cannot. And so, rather than simply allowing these utterly unfounded accusations to die on the vine of bitter grapes from whence they were wrung, I have decided to take my case to the public.

First of all, let me state emphatically that I have not read Mr. Grinn's book,[iii] nor do I intend to do so. However, I did recently receive a copy of the so-called "jest" I allegedly plagiarized in the mail, and I was frankly shocked that anyone could have given Mr. Grinn's complaints a forum (as did the *New York Post* and the website *Galley Cat,* among others).

Mind you, I am not saying that there aren't some similarities between our pieces—the limited conventions of the comic story virtually guarantee it—but I am saying that viewed in whole, rather than in carefully selected "excerpts," it becomes clear that there is precious little to link our work and far more that distinguishes it. To wit:

1) "Just the other day, I was having a drink." All of the stories in the *Treasury,* including the one from which these opening remarks were allegedly lifted, are told in the third person. My story, on the other hand, is a first-person narrative, making it less a jest than an anecdote. Grinn's episode is also cast in the past tense, while mine moves imperceptibly from past to present, an experimental-fiction technique that lends the piece a contemporariness that Grinn's entire volume lacks.

2) "Mulligan's Brew over on Forty-Third Street." A detail curiously missing from the supposedly purloined text.

3) "Pink-and-purple kangaroo." An intensely personal allusion to my own

---

iii. In the interest of full disclosure, I must point out that I met Mr. Grinn once, at a 2005 *New York* magazine party celebrating the magazine's "100 Wittiest New Yorkers." (No, I didn't make the list, but I do not have the good fortune of being a client of Leslee Dart, as were a striking sixty-three of our city's wittiest, including Mr. Grinn.) I cannot recall if Mr. Grinn told the joke in dispute at this gathering, as I was, to be perfectly frank, quite drunk. I was also unaware that Mr. Grinn was married, or that Marie was his wife.

During our subsequent time together, Marie never related to me Mr. Grinn's precious joke, or, for that matter, any precious jest belonging to her former husband, whom she found to be dour and petty, and who never made her laugh. She is willing to sign an affidavit to this effect.

childhood, predating the *Treasury* by a good twenty years, and giving the whole a surreal quality that Grinn's garden-variety kangaroo fails to provoke.

4) "Barkeep, give me a Screaming Orgasm." Note the wording in the Grinn version: "Bartender, I'd like a Piña Colada." A Screaming Orgasm is not only a more contemporary reference, but it frames the entire episode in a double-entendre context, making it more of an adult tale, in stark contrast to Grinn's rather childlike prose.

5) "So [the bartender, when asked how much the drink costs,] says, 'Twenty bucks.'" In Grinn's version, it is only five dollars—a small detail perhaps, but try this joke out on a New York audience using the lower figure and see how many people appreciate the hyperbole.

6) "[The kangaroo] hops off his stool to leave." A mere flourish, admittedly, yet like many others throughout the piece, a telling one.

7) Note the clear difference in cadence between "We've never had a talking kangaroo in here before" (Grinn version) and "We've never had a talking pink-and-purple kangaroo in here before"(Doyle version).

8) In the final analysis, the real proof is in the punch line. Grinn: "'I'm not surprised,' the kangaroo angrily retorted, 'and if you keep charging five dollars for a Piña Colada, you won't have any others, I'll tell you that.'" Doyle: "'Well,' the kangaroo says. 'At twenty bucks for one lousy Screaming Orgasm, I'm not a bit surprised.'" In addition to its aforementioned contemporary and ribald qualities, my version is certainly more parsimonious than Grinn's run-at-the-mouth gagism. Further, it displays that ineffable quality that separates the ridiculous from the sublime, a chuckle from a guffaw—*timing*.

I could go on, but I think I'll leave the relentless self-posturing to Mr. Grinn. And to those who still believe his reckless charges of plagiarism, I can think of no more appropriate response than to quote something my university creative writing teacher, Mark Costello, once told me.

"Larry," he said, "always remember: mediocre writers borrow; great writers steal."

ANGELS MAY REPLACE VAMPIRES
AS NEW TREND IN TEEN LIT

—*Huffington Post*

Notes on My Next Bestseller

Weirdest dream. Must get this down.

Angel floating over my bed. Very buff, but also vulnerable somehow. Long flowing locks, but his face and body hairless. Smells like chocolate.

Angel says unto me: "I am love but cannot love."

I say back: "What?"

Angel says: "I have so much love to give some lost young woman, but alas, I cannot indulge in the carnal."

I say: "Okay."

He says: "You can use that."

Rereading this in the morning. What was he trying to tell me?

Epiphany: *Hot sexy angel wants to make sweet celestial love to you but cannot.* This is big!

Reading Bible for insp. No angels so far. In two thousand years, they couldn't compile an index?

Possible titles: *Angels and Dames. Fallen Love.* Keep thinking on this.

Finally: Genesis 19:1: *"And there came two angels to Sodom at even."*

Man, God is *mean.*

Why can't Angels have sex with teenage girls? Need strong, dramatic, yet plausible reason. Sex makes them mortal? It turns the girls into demons, or swans? No genitalia?

Because God said so!

Hot sexy angel who wants to make sweet celestial love to you but *it is forbidden.* Yes!

Exodus 3:2: *"And the angel of the Lord appeared unto him in a flame of fire out of the midst of a bush."* That is sexy. Been used?

"Heavensent." "Angelophilia."

2 Kings 19:35: *"And it came to pass that night, that the angel of the Lord went out, and smote in the camp of the Assyrians an hundred fourscore and five thousand: and when they arose early in the morning, behold, they were all dead corpses."* Digging a dry hole here. Need better source material.

"A Coming of Angels." But will people get it? Might keep me out of libraries, and Texas. "A Kissing of Angels."

Went to B&N and asked if they had any books on angels. A whole floor! I'm on to something here.

Seraphim? Cherubim? Ophanim? Malakhim? How am I supposed to keep all those straight?

Clerk says if I tear pages out of a book, I have to buy it. She suggested I try Google.

Jesus Christ!

Ninety-two million hits! If only half buy my book @ $25, I'm a billionaire!

Shouldn't get bogged down in research. That's not what puts it on the iPad. Use my imagination! If God can create the heavens and the earth in six days—fun fact—I can create a hot and sexy teen angel romance before the electricity goes out.

Opening image: *A glorious well-oiled angel riding on a winged unicorn.* Sure, it's sexy. But *too* sexy?

Divine inspiration: *Mangel.*

"Raging Mangel." "My Mangel." "Heaven Sent Me a Mangel." "The Mangel Chronicles." I smell franchise!

Damn. "Mangel" already trademarked for another purpose.

The work's the thing. Build it and the title will come.

Need a villain. Satan too obvious. Werewolves would be interesting, but maybe not formidable enough. The Catholic Church? Could work.

Big Business! Evil developer wants to build over an ancient Christian burial site. Forest Lawn! Sexy angels sitting on the Hollywood Sign! All coming together.

Hmm. Sounds vaguely familiar.

Of course. Change Forest Lawn to the Greenwich Village crypt of Dracula's sexy undead son, Liam, and the Hollywood Sign to the Washington Square Arch, and it's my woefully misunderstood young adult bodice-and-neck ripper, *Hot Wings.*

Hallelujah!

"This is the funeral pyre for thought in America today,"
Mr. Wayne told spectators as he lighted the first batch
from the warehouse where he has gathered thousands
of books in the 10 years he has run the store, Prospero's
Books. When Mr. Wayne sought to thin out the collection,
he said, he found that he could not even give the books
away to libraries and bookshops, which said they were
full. So, he said, he began burning the books to protest
society's diminishing support for the printed word.

—*New York Times*

The Hot Book

Where am I? The Vegas Book Show? San Diego Litcon? Have I made
it to the end, to Powell's, at long last?

"You're in Cleveland," Alison says. "Barnes & Noble Arena."

Cleveland? How can I be in Cleveland? Wasn't I just in St. Louis?

"We had to move a couple things around to get out of Collin's way." The *Mockingjay* tour, in its sixieth week. Two dozen singing, dancing, battling teens. Why can't she just read the damn book, like the rest of us?

"Drink me," I say, only half alluding. Alison pours us two Absolut Writinis (8 oz. Absolut in a coffee mug with an Altoid chaser), courtesy of our tour sponsor. I fish my right hand out of the bucket and reach for my medicine. "*Back in the bucket,*" Alison says, all marm, pressing the mug into my left. I return my right to the ice water, where it now lives. It's not even my hand anymore; it's ballooned into a monstrous cartoon of a hand, Homer Simpson's mitt. It lies quietly on the bottom like a strange aquatic animal. (Not bad. I'll have to use that.)

The chanting. Rhythmic, primal, it begins:

REE-ding . . . REE-ding . . . REE-ding!

"Al," I say, finishing my drink. "I don't think I can do this tonight."

She sighs. Alison's a seasoned tour pro and has heard this before, from me, from DeLillo, from all the chicks with lits. "You've got twenty thousand people out there, some paid scalpers three hundred bucks to come hear you read," she preaches from the playbook. "Not to mention what they spent on T-shirts, and readings CDs, and giant foam bookmarks. . . ."

"They're not even laughing at the jokes anymore. They're laughing at the punctuation."

"Your punctuation *is* funny."

"So many people. Such long names."

"You're lucky it's not a memoir," Alison says. "They'd tear you apart." Poor choice of words, I think, considering this very stadium held the last reading of James Frey, somewhat ironically torn into only eighty-seven little pieces.

Ree-ding!... Ree-ding!!... Ree-ding!!!

I hoist out what used to be my writing hand. "It's dead," I pronounce.

"Marty," Alison says.

Dr. Marty, the tour physician, shuffles over. He lays my bloated corpse of a paw across his lap. He pokes it. "Boy's right," the doc says in his syrupy Staten Island drawl. "This thing's about to fall off."

"If I wanted your medical opinion, I would have asked for it," Alison snaps.

The good doctor nods and reaches into his bag, removing his fixings. He pops the syringe into the vial, pulls back on the plunger, and slowly withdraws a potent cocktail of vitamin B, morphine, and Major League Baseball–grade steroids. He taps my wrist twice and plunges the needle in. I don't even feel it.

"This got Updike through the *Couples* tour," Dr. Marty says. "You think it's bad now. Back then they not only bought the books, they *read* them."

Outside, the crowd has gone into an undulating roar. They are doing the wave, apparently.

"We better get you in there," Alison says. "We don't want another San Antonio." *The Last Symbol* fiasco. Dan Brown's flight was delayed. Before he could be helicoptered in, eight people were dead and posed ritualistically.

As I climb into the golf cart, I notice something on Fox News. People. Anger. Flames.

They're all throwing my book into the fire. I could tell because of the distinctive cover.

I had said a stupid thing. The reporter showed me one of the full-page ads my publisher had taken out in newspapers across the country, quoting some blogger calling my novel "the greatest book ever written." Surely, the reporter asked, I didn't think my book was *better than the Bible.*

"It's funnier than the Bible," I said.

And I believe that. The Bible isn't funny at all, except in a broad conceptual way. But I shouldn't have said it, probably.

There are bonfires going in twenty-six cities, Megyn Kelly says, and on a couple of cruise ships. I stare at the screen. My words, on fire. My lovely books, thousands of them, turning to ash.

I chuckle. They didn't even get a volume discount.

The cart comes out of the tunnel into what was once center field. The crowd roars and squeals in equal measure. They have come for the word. And I'm going to read it to them.

Last fall in an attic in Hollywood, two sisters rifling through their grandfather's things came upon an item their ancestor had borrowed from the Buffalo and Erie County Public Library more than a century before. It was perhaps the most infamous overdue book of all time: the first half of Mark Twain's original manuscript for The Adventures of Huckleberry Finn, *665 handwritten pages containing many passages omitted from the final version and thought to be lost forever. Because of the inherent literary, cultural, and historic value of the manuscript, the sisters immediately asked Sotheby's in New York to sell it for as much as possible. The library, in turn, hired a powerful phalanx of big-city lawyers, demanding immediate return of the manuscript and payment of fines exceeding one million dollars (fifteen cents per day, compounded at 6 percent annually). It may be years before the matter is resolved.*

Nevertheless, Sire *magazine has managed to obtain, at great expense (and, we hasten to add, well outside the borders of the United States), a high-resolution facsimile copy of the manuscript. While a number of pages appear to have been eaten by the fax machine, what came through intact is a literary find indeed. As the magazine which first published* Huckleberry Finn *in serial form, beginning in the fall of 1876 (under the unfortunate title* A Boy and His Boy*), we are proud to present to our readers never-before-seen excerpts from this satiric masterpiece. Critical commentary and annotation have been provided by* Sire *literary editor Laurence Doyle, who has read much of Mr. Twain's work and considers himself a great fan.*

Huck of Darkness

Mark Twain's *The Adventures of Huckleberry Finn* is, above all else, a classic coming-of-age story about a young boy's search for his identity.[1] It is also, according to the critic Leslie Fiedler, a sort of literary "fairy tale" celebrating "the mutual love *of a white man and a colored*."[2] But the recent discovery of the first half of Twain's

---

1. See also Larry Doyle's "Huck Finn's Search for His Identity," a five-page, double-spaced monograph, Advanced Composition II, Ms. Rosenbaum, Rm. A113, February 1974.
2. See Fiedler's "Come Back to the Raft Ag'in, Huck Honey!" which first appeared in *Partisan Review,* June 1948, but which also provides the text for a new one-man show starring Terrence Howard, currently playing in Key West in the Tennessee Williams Theater's upper mezzanine men's room.

handwritten manuscript[3] indicates that *Finn,* in its original form, is in fact something else again: a veritable treasure trove of zany "lost episodes"[4] to be enjoyed and analyzed by scholars and casual readers alike.[5]

Three such episodes are presented on the following pages. In order to place these passages in their proper context, readers are encouraged to cut them out and paste them, in the appropriate places, into their own copies of *Huck Finn,*[6] and then reread the entire book from start to finish.

EPISODE ONE:
PAP GOES THE WEASEL

As described in the opening chapters of the novel, Huck's relationship with his father is a troubled one. A typical father-son interaction cycle between Huck and his "pap"[7] involves: Pap bullying Huck for money to buy liquor; Pap getting drunk; Pap going to jail; Pap

---

3. See *Sire,* Vol. 12, No. 130, italicized introduction, above.

4. The phrase "zany 'lost episodes'" does not appear in the original draft of this article and was apparently added for "commercial reasons" over the objections of the author. The author's intended locution, which should be restored in future editions, was "*Finn*-tastic philological finds."

5. Although these two groups are not mutually exclusive, as longtime readers of this magazine are well aware. See especially Norman Mailer's "Mammarian Signifying: The Ironic Nipple," foreword to *Sire's This Is Booberama!* (1977), a book of photographic essays.

6. Librarians please note: unauthorized copying is illegal. However, additional copies of this magazine can be purchased at newsstands and bookstores across the country.

7. Pike County dialect for "father," possibly derived from the Euro-Mediterranean "papa" or Middle-American "pop."

getting out of jail; and, finally, Pap beating the tar out of Huck, often leaving him "all over welts."[8] While such behavior is now easily recognized as symptomatic of an extremely dysfunctional codependency, at the time it was merely considered a form of child abuse, to be frowned upon rather than understood in terms of how it might affect both parties. Clearly, Twain meant to satirize this simplistic notion and wanted to say more about the nature of Huck's relationship with his father; and in fact he did.

Near the end of chapter VI, there is a curious omission from the classic "delirium tremens" episode in which Pap, intoxicated,[9] believes himself covered with snakes and demons and then attacks Huck. The passage speaks for itself. (Excised material appears in bold type.)

He chased me round and round the place, with a clasp-knife, calling me the Angel of Death and saying he would kill me and then I couldn't come for him no more. I begged, and told him I was only Huck, but he laughed such a screechy laugh, **it sent an awful scare through me and I froze up long enough that he could catch me and shove me down on the ground.**

My face was in the dirt then and he lay atop me, press-

---

8. Huck's self-report.

9. Based on Huck's anecdotal evidence, medical authorities believe Pap's blood-alcohol content may have been between 0.21 and 0.24, more than double the level required to have him arrested for drunk driving, had automobiles been invented and had he been driving one at the time, although the technology to determine this was not yet available during the period in which this incident takes place, and so we must take Huck's (and Twain's) word for it that Pap was, in fact, intoxicated.

ing with all his weight and with his liquory breath burning wet on the back of my neck. I figgered I was guv up for ghost for sure then. But pap he just flopped on me for awhile, all fagged out, and I got to hoping maybe he had forgot what he was there for. But he didn't. By and by, he got himself up on his knees, straddling my hindparts, but swaying uneasy, and made out how he would cut off my angel wings to show as a warning to other angels that might come after him. Before I could figure on a good plan to stop him, I began crying like a babe, uncontrollable:

"I hain't a angel, Pappy! I hain't no angel! I'm only your own flesh and blood, Huck Finn, your son!"

I don't know if it was me bawling or pap not finding no wings to cut off me, but he stopped poking at my back with the knife and rolled me over front to have a look at me. He kept squatting on my chest, though, and pinned my arms under his knees, in case of if I was one of those deceiving angels, he said. He stared hard at me for the longest while, and when he smiled I thought maybe the spell had gone off him. But then he started talking all crazy again, sing-songy:

"M'boy-M'boy-M'boy. My sweetscented dandy boy, ain't you now? Why, y'got your mama's mouth, y'kno'that? Yes, y'got her perty dirty li'l' mouth."

He began fumbling with his belt then, and I knew what that meant: I was in for a licking. But I thought quick and bellowed in the darkest, devilest voice I had in me:

"Haw! I am the Angel of Death, you foolish ol' man! and now I'm gone drag you into the Eternal Fires of Hell!"

Well, pap's eyeballs went black as new moons and he

just yanked himself up by his britches, and fell over in a tumble. He roared and cussed, **got to his feet** and kept on chasing me up.

It is unclear why Twain chose to drop this episode, although it is likely that Olivia Clemens, Twain's wife and editrix, would have objected to the use of the word "hell" in the penultimate graph and deleted the curse.[10] Perhaps Twain felt the passage would not work without it.

This excision notwithstanding, Twain did leave several other clues to Pap's nontraditional sexuality in his final draft, particularly in the scene in which Nigger[11] Jim and Huck find Pap dead and "Yes, indeedy; *naked,* too" (emphasis mine) in a house floating down the river. Jim warns Huck "doan' look at his face—it's too gashly," to which Huck responds, "I didn't look at him at all. . . . I didn't want to see him." Huck does, however, take an almost fetishistic interest in the contents of the house:

> There was . . . a couple of masks made out of black cloth . . . two old dirty calico dresses, and a sun-bonnet, and some women's under-clothes . . . a fish-line as thick as my little finger with

10. While Olivia was diligent in patrolling Twain's work for strong language, his sexual allusions often went right by her. See, for example, Twain's *Roughing It*.

11. Much has been written elsewhere about why Twain chose this ethnic nomenclature over the currently acceptable "African American" (See "Longhome [*sic*] Clemens: Racist Devil," an anonymous Black paper distributed free at libraries, airports, and bus depots), but in Twain's defense, it should be noted that, at the time, everybody called them niggers.

some monstrous hooks on it, and a roll of buckskin, and a leather dog collar. . . .

Huck takes all these items with him. They will later play "a very important part in the plot of the novel *Huckleberry Finn,* which is really about Huck's search for his identity."[12]

EPISODE TWO:
HUCKLEBERRY PIE

Certainly no one factor is more important in Huck's coming of age than his relationship with Nigger Jim. It is Jim who encourages Huck to explore all sides of his burgeoning identity; for example, in chapter X, when Huck wants to sneak across the river after dark to catch up on gossip, Huck relates:

Jim liked that notion; . . . he studied it over and said, couldn't I put on some of them old things and dress up like a girl?

Huck enthusiastically complies, and while such transvestism is quite common and normal among teenage boys,[13] Huck appears genuinely concerned about getting accurately in touch with his feminine side:

I practiced around all day to get the hang of the things, and by and by I could do pretty well in them, only Jim said I didn't walk like a girl. . . . I took notice, and done better.

---

12. Doyle, op. cit.
13. Ask anybody.

Of course, all Huck's prancing goes for nought; the woman he visits quickly sees "Sarah Williams" for the confused young boy he is (Huck doesn't "throw like a girl"). In the published novel, the episode ends here, a mere burlesque; but as the manuscript makes clear, Twain fully intended Huck's "walk on the wild side" to have more psychosexual import.[14]

In the manuscript, the woman's husband arrives home before Huck can make his escape. Despite Huck's and the woman's protestations, the man insists on escorting "Sarah" home "on account of he said he wouldn't be able to sleep knowing such an innocent thing as me was wandering in them dark evil woods unprotected." In the passage that follows, Huck learns an important lesson about gender bending and indeed about life.

We walked into the woods a ways and he kept trying to talk me up: where'd I get the perty dress? did I have a beau? did I have any older brothers? But I didn't answer exactly, just tittered and giggled, so as to not be discovered again.

About a half mile in, I turned to the man and I says, all girlish:

"Thank you very kindly, sir, I can make my own way from here. You've taken me far enough already."

---

14. An early editor of this article suggested replacing the phrase "psychosexual import" with the word "oomph," arguing that the author's use of the former amounted to "soporific pedantry," a characterization the author subsequently deemed "masturbatory fustianism," precipitating a heated exchange of rhetorical devices and body blows. Please note the final wording.

"Yep," the man said, looking round.

"Reckon we is gone far enough, alrighty."

Then the man, as casual as can be, plucked off his hat and dropped it to the ground. He says:

"Sarah Williams, would y'bend over an' pick up my hat fer me, like a good girl? I hain't got the back for it."

I smelt a lie, but I saw he had a gun, and so I bent over, as womanlike as I could.

I can't rightly say what happened next, or leastwise I won't. But I will say this man weren't near as clever as his missus: a lucky thing, too, seeing as he would've killed me if he figured out I warn't no girl. But he didn't, maybe since I squawked and carried on just like a girl would, though that weren't hard on account of it hurt so much. It made me wonder, though, why do womenfolk have any business to do with us men atall? I know if I was ever a girl it'd take a good sight more than some old gold band to get me to cleave unto my husband, no matter what any Good Book had to say about the thing.

Well, the man finished up his cleaving soon enough, and left me there to find my own way home. He weren't worried about my innocence no more, I reckon.

Again, it is unclear why Twain allowed this passage to be dropped from the final publication.[15] But whatever the reason, it

---

15. One might speculate that Twain did not wish to be jailed as a pornographer, but there is little documentary evidence to support this. In fact, *Sire* had already published far more explicit material two years earlier, when it serialized the long-suppressed final book of C. Dodgson's childhood trilogy, *Down My Trousers; and What Alice Fond There.*

is unfortunate, as this episode proves to be an important turning point in Huck's life: it is the moment Huck realizes he must throw off the girlish frills of his youth and become a man.

EPISODE THREE:
HUCK'S "DREAM"

Much has been made previously of the "Raftsmen's Passage,"[16] a fifteen-page episode which appears in the 1876 *Finn* manuscript (between the second and third paragraphs of chapter XVI), but which was deleted prior to final publication after being used to pad out *Life on the Mississippi,* a book written to cover Twain's losses from an ill-considered attempt to mount "The Celebrated Jumping Frog of Calaveras County" as an "All-Singin', All Jumpin'" traveling minstrel show. But while it can be argued that this Raftsmen's Passage, in which Huck observes some raftsmen, is an insignificant event in Huck's development, as well as tedious in the extreme, the same certainly cannot be said of the recently discovered "Dream Sequence," deleted from the previous chapter (chapter XV) for quite different reasons.

Chapter XV begins:

> We judged that three more nights would fetch us to Cairo, at the bottom of Illinois, where the Ohio River comes in, and that was what we was after. We would sell the raft and get on a steamboat and go way up the Ohio amongst the free States, and then be out of trouble.
>
> Well, the second night . . .

---

16. You can Google it just as well as I can.

Clearly something is missing here: namely, the first night. It must be remembered that Twain was being paid a then-astounding seventeen cents a word by *Sire*, and it was certainly not in his character to pass up an unnecessary narrative opportunity.[17] And in point of fact, he did not:

There weren't much to do in that first night but smoke and talk, which is what we was doing when Jim said why didn't we make a party of it and suck on pap's jug some? I said I didn't think that was a good idea, on account of we wasn't sick or pained, but Jim says:

"Wud's de harm in it, Huck? A man doan' need no caws t'be feelin' good. Ain't you a man like yo' pap, Huck?"

I didn't want to argue him none on *that* point, so I tipped the jug and swallered once. That was plenty. The stuff burnt so bad I thought maybe I had set it afire with my pipe by accident and that there was smoke apouring out of my ears and eyes. Jim decided this was the funniest sight he'd ever seen, and laughed so hard he fell over sideways; I would've cussed him out if I could've talked at all, but instead took another swig of my medicine, like a man.

---

17. One story, possibly apocryphal, relates that the first installment of *Finn*, as submitted to *Sire*, originally began, "You don't know about me without you have read a book by the name of 'The Adventures of Tom Sawyer'; so here might be a good place for me to tell you what happened in that one before I take up with this one," followed by a six-thousand-word summary of Sawyer from Huck's point of view. According to magazine legend, founding editor Peter Van Oppenclause red-penciled everything after "Tom Sawyer," replacing it with the now more familiar "but that ain't no matter."

Well, by and by it didn't so much burn as make me feel
all warm inside, and I got the sudden urge to lay back on
the raft and look up at the sky. It was such a clear night and
there was a sight more stars than usual, and friskier, too.
This got me to thinking. I says:

"Jim, Jim—hey, Jim—do you think they's niggers up in
heaven?"

Jim puzzled over this for a moment, and then he said:

"I reck'n dey is, Huck, I do reck'n so. De man, wun't he
be wantin' his nigger up dah wid him in hivven? or it wun't
right' be hivven now, wud it?"

I said I reckoned he was correct about that, that was
smart thinking. But then I thought: Jim being a runaway
nigger, how was he ever going to get into heaven? Just the
thought of being dead and not having Jim to talk to me
made me so lonesome I wanted to cry, but I must of fell
asleep instead.

I had this powerful horrible dream then. I dreamed
I had gone down to the bad place, and there was all over
demons and witches and burnt runaway niggers, and I
was crying on account I didn't know what I had done to be
there. Then I was in this tiny room, more like the inside of
a stove than a room, and this demon come walking toward
me. It was pap, *red as the devil himself*!

Pap was grabbing at this big spikey tail he had, and
was swinging it over his head when, by witch magic, it
turned into a terrible spitting snake. He was grinning just
like he did that one night and kept coming at me, asking
wouldn't I like to touch his snake? I said, no thank you just

the same.[18] He said, my, didn't I have the dandy manners, maybe he should learn me some other manners about respecting my elders and doing what they say, and he kept coming on, and just when his snake was about to bite me, I woke up in a thick sweat.

I felt sick. My heart was beating like a jackrabbit; my face was redhot and my body all ashiver, and I didn't know what to do. I tried to sit up quick but something held me flat. I looked down, and there was ol' Jim, bending over them parts of me that Judge Thatcher said was so private and sacred even I had no business with them, and all of a sudden it made final and horrible sense to me: Jim was a night vampyre coming to suck out my immortal soul!

I tried to escape his niggery fangs, but it was too late. I felt a jerking all down my back and an awful itch in my belly and my soul started shooting out of me like a steamboat whistle; the devil Jim was laughing like a banshee and sucking it all up! I felt my body go all tingly and then I reckon I must of passed out from the fright.

I didn't wake up the next morning until near about eight o'clock, and Jim was there sitting next to me, swabbing my brow with a soaked rag. He says:

"Easy dah, easy, chile. It's jis' dem bad whisky dreams is all. You be 'right en fine; I reck'n you gwyne get t' likin' it, too, you en'thin' like yo' pap. Y'suh; you is a man now, Huck."

---

18. Huck's superstitious aversion to snakes is a recurring theme in the book. In chapter X, for example, Huck swears he "wouldn't ever take aholt of a skin again with my hands, now that I see what come of it." And yet, as this passage makes clear, he can't seem to avoid them.

Is this the smoking "naked sword" of which Fiedler wrote, or was the whole episode, as Jim claims, just an adolescent wet dream? Any suggestion of the latter is dispelled the very next night, when Huck and Jim are separated for many hours in a dense fog. In the published work, Huck describes feeling "dismal and lonesome," and when finally reunited with Jim, Jim exclaims:

> Goodness gracious, is dat you, Huck? . . . It's too good for true, honey, it's too good for true. Lemme look at you, chile, lemme feel o' you. . . .

Huck, however, cannot resist playing a boyish prank on Jim, pretending the entire separation has been a dream.[19] This precipitates what is probably the most famous lovers' tiff in literary history:

> " . . . En when I wake up en fine you back agin, all safe en soun', de tears come en I could a got down on my knees en kiss yo' foot[20] I's so thankful. En all you wuz thinkin 'bout wuz how you could make a fool uv ole Jim wid a lie. . . ."

---

19. When Huck tells Jim, "You couldn't a got drunk . . . so of course you've been dreaming," he is making a sly reference to the previous evening, a reference that readers, until now, have been unable to enjoy. It is difficult to imagine how much more satisfying this passage, and consequently the entire novel, might have been had the Dream Sequence been intact from the very beginning. The book very well might have sold better, and Twain would not have been forced, as he was in later life, to write for television.

20. Twain apparently chose several other words before settling on this one, but they are too heavily marked out to be deciphered.

Then he got up slow, and walked to the wigwam, and went in there, without saying anything but that. But that was enough. It made me feel so mean I could almost kissed his foot[21] to get him to take it[22] back.

It was fifteen minutes before I could work myself up to go and humble myself to a nigger—but I done it, and I warn't ever sorry for it afterwards, neither.

Clearly, then, the lost Dream Sequence is an integral, some might say crucial, event in Huck's coming-of-age. But if so, why was it omitted? Sadly, the fault may lie with this very magazine. A search behind our files has turned up the following undated letter written to Twain by editor Schuyler Livingston Newburyport Schenk, probably between late summer or early fall 1876.

Dear Sam,

Thank you for sending along the most recent installment of "A Boy and His Boy," but I am afraid we are going to have to pass on this one. I know we asked you to "spice it up a bit," but some of us here felt that perhaps you stepped over the line separating spice from perversion. I am sorry to disappoint you.

I do, however, have one suggestion, and please feel free to disregard it if it is not in keeping with what you intended for this piece. We thought that perhaps this sequence would work better, and be more palatable to our readers, if Nigger Jim were instead a

---

21. Again, as above. In a couple of instances, Twain's alternative wordings are so vigorously edited that he actually tore a hole in the manuscript.
22. "Me" in the original draft.

Negress Jemima. It is our feeling that if you made the switch now,
very few readers would notice, and you could revise the earlier
installments accordingly should you ever wish to put this together
as a book.

Please let me know what you think.
All the best.

Twain immediately broke off correspondence with *Sire* and
put the manuscript aside for nearly two years. Unable to write, he
traveled to Europe, where he struck up a friendship with a Vien-
nese medical intern named Sigmund Freud. A series of long con-
versations with the young physician apparently freed Twain of his
writer's block, and he returned to America, eager to "finish that
damnable book, and make it Huck's, not my own."[23]

Of course, by that time he was well behind in his deadlines
for *Sire*,[24] and was compelled to write the last twenty-eight chap-
ters of *Huckleberry Finn* over a concentrated two-week period,[25]
giving the latter half of the book that "dashed-off" quality about
which many critics have rightly complained.

---

23. Manufactured quotation.

24. And in fact, he missed several installments altogether; these were supplied
    by contributing editor Charles Dickens, who, as usual, needed the money.
    Twain was either too proud to allow these episodes to appear in his book or
    could not come to terms with Dickens, but these outrageously entertaining
    Finn chapters later supplied the inspiration for Dickens's minor master-
    piece *Beast House*.

25. During which he reportedly slept at the magazine's offices, not bathing
    once. Some say Twain's aura still lingers there to this day.

Merriment

Let's Talk About My New Movie

It's about more than an alien invasion, or a big dance contest, although if you're a fan of invading aliens or professional choreography you won't be disappointed. It's also a love story, born of deep space and lived on an underwater dance floor; and it's about the characters: the hero, the babe, the bad guy, the black guy, the guy who was funny when he was on *SNL*, and others. More than anything, though, it's about freedom—the idea of freedom as opposed to any specific exercise of it—and liberty, which is a different word from "liberal," and about the special effects, which are more special than ever before, and Crest Whitestrips, which—SPOILER ALERT—save humanity.

I hesitate to call it a remake, for legal reasons but also because what I think we're doing here is not so much remaking or reimagining as reimagineering™, if I may coin and trademark a term. This is really a film for people who weren't alive seven years ago to see the original, or who were drunk and barely remember it, or who can't tell one movie from another anymore. It's for all those people, and their dates.

Make no mistake: we're not trying to replace the original, except in the marketplace. The original is still out there somewhere, in whatever form existed back then, as is the television show on which it was based, or its previous incarnation as a comic book inspired by a toy. The toy, of course, is no longer available, but we have a new toy, one that I am confident will prove to be not nearly as deadly, while retaining much of the original's play value.

Some members of the media have pointed out that our story contains eerie parallels to the current situation, and that's their job, I guess—to scare away potential moviegoers, at least when they're not pawing through my garbage, their tiny red eyes caught in the glare of my security lights, their pointy yellow teeth flecked with coffee grounds and dripping rancid goo, possibly separated butter. But I digress.

I honestly can't tell you how much of our movie is based on the current situation. I'm not an expert. But I can assure you our movie is far more entertaining than the current situation, whatever it may be. And that it was never our intention to take sides in any political debate, military conflict, or national catastrophe but simply to exploit these similarities in a positive way. Nor are we hoping that people will think about the movie once they leave the theater. The sooner they forget about it the better, because the DVD is coming out in two weeks.

I'd like to take a moment here to address these rumors about Kendra and me. Whatever we did or did not do, in whose trailer, together or in tandem, or at what angle, is between the two of us and a very small crew. In any case, my publicist has vehemently denied everything, and that's good enough for me.

Whether Kendra is pregnant with my child, whether they're twins and only one of them is mine, whether she's actually carrying alien spawn in yet another eerie parallel to the film—that's for her people to deny, vehemently, categorically, or otherwise. That sonogram on the Internet looks nothing like me, more like a peeled shrimp or that one camera guy.

As for the rumors about Jacob, what have you heard?

I won't deny it was a tough shoot. There were some heated arguments on the set, with subsequent gunplay, but this is typical of any creative endeavor where there are a bunch of guns just left lying around.

In the end, I have to say, it was worth it. It's an excellent entertainment product. Of course, I can't take all of the credit. Much of that must contractually go to the director, as well as the lead actor and actress, their stunt and body doubles, the hair and makeup people, the incredible crew, everyone's agents and managers, and the dozens of immensely talented writers who contributed words to the project. But when it comes to the triple-shot caramel macchiatos that kept the lead actor awake, the soy lattes that kept the lead actress from starving, and the black-with-three-Equals-and-not-the-same-goddamn-thing-in-a-different-packet that kept the director from screaming at everyone, I'd like to think I had some small part in that.

We have an obligation, as broadcasters, to satisfy the
appetites of the American public.

—Former Fox Television chairman Sandy Grushow

You Asked for It

| 2 | **The Quest** No-rules scavenger hunt in which contestants race to steal priceless artifacts from exotic foreign locales. Tonight: The Bones of Saint Matthew. *Piracy* |
| 4 | **Pants on Fire** Contestants with pants set on fire must race to douse their behinds in a single barrel full of water. *Prankedy* |

5	**Yesteryear** One hundred contestants live in a small town where kids catch crawdads and egg creams cost a nickel; elimination determined by lottery. *Competitive Nostalgia* (TV-PG: Stonings)
7	**Doghouse** Husbands compete to do nice things for their wives. *Unscripted Domcom*
13	**Great Performances** The New York Philharmonic performs music from popular YouTube videos.
CNN	**Box Populi** Ordinary people are offered the opportunity to punch newsmakers in the face. Tonight: Vice President Joe Biden. *Public Service*
CSPAN	**Congress After Dark**
DISCOVERY	**Whoa, Science!** Researchers burn ants with magnifying glass.
FOOD	**Lingerie Models Eat Chocolate Cake with Their Hands**
GAME	**The Pain Game** Contestants stab each other with shrimp forks.
LIFE	**Adorable Babies**
NICK	**Bang!** Kids shoot cats and stuff with semiautomatic weapons.
MSNBC	**Capitol Buzz** Elected officials give frank answers to viewers' questions or receive increasingly painful electric shocks. *Politcom*
MTV	**Totally Banned Videos** Uncut versions of videos banned by MTV. Tonight: Lady Gaga's "Taste My Ass."

TLC	**Corpus Celebri** Autopsies of recently deceased celebrities or their victims. *Morbidity*
TRU	**Spread the Wealth** Mobs of contestants roam wealthy neighborhoods, beating residents for cash, jewelry, and other prizes. *Rioting*
WGN	**Monkeys Fucking**

The Larry Doyle Story As Told to Larry Doyle

FOR IMMEDIATE RELEASE

LOS ANGELES, NEW YORK, and LONDON—"Laughing" Larry Doyle, in conjunction with LD Associates and LarDo Ltd., proudly announces that principal photography has begun on *Laughing All the Way: The Larry Doyle Story,* a major feature film based on the soon-to-be-released bestseller *Laughing All the Way Home: My Own Story,* written by Larry Doyle under a grant from the Larry Doyle Group.

The $200 million film is being produced and directed by Larry Doyle, who will play all the major roles in the film, with the exception of his best friend and sidekick, who will be played by Larry Doyle's real life best friend and sidekick, to be announced.

Larry Doyle will also sing the title song, the achingly funny "Larry's Laugh," in a duet with himself harmonizing in a slightly higher register.

Larry Doyle's acting-writing-directing-and-producing debut represents the first time more than $200 million has been spent on a comedy starring a novice in so many roles. But Larry-Doyle-

Artist Co., which has agreed to distribute *LATW: The Larry Doyle Story,* says it is confident the feature will earn back the $240 million even before it officially opens, "and if not, it has been an honor being part of this truly important—and very, very funny—film."

All told, Larry Doyle will have sixty-three speaking roles in *LATW: The Larry Doyle Story,* and will appear in every scene an average of 7.8 times. Making these tour-de-"farce" performances possible will be HolosoftVR™, a soon-to-be-cutting-edge process that combines computer animation, holographics, and Muppetry. Unlike recent multiple-role comedies, which required the actors to respond to tennis balls on sticks, HolosoftVR™ will allow Larry Doyle to interact directly with adorable soft cotton copies of himself. While the technology—developed by Larry Doyle working with Henson's Creatures Shop under a grant from the Department of Defense—is untested, sources on the set report the only difficulty so far has been Larry Doyle "cracking himself up," forcing some scenes to be reshot several times, albeit "each take funnier than the one before."

In *LATW: The Larry Doyle Story,* Larry Doyle portrays himself at ages five, eight, twelve, sixteen, and as an adult—a particularly keen acting challenge, since his only previous acting experience was in an untitled Egyptian sketch in the fifth grade. But Larry Doyle more than rises to the occasion: using self-hypnosis, he regresses into each of his younger selves, and actually *relives* harrowing and heartwarming scenes from his childhood before the camera, still managing to find the essential funniness of each. To complete the cinematic transformation, the early Larry Doyle scenes are the first ever to be shot using Encephaloscope™, which selectively shrinks the head and the rest of the body, producing more childlike proportions. As evidence of Larry Doyle's commitment to his craft, it should be noted that Encephaloscope™ is not a photographic process but a medical procedure.

Moreover, in order to prepare for the roles of his father and mother—Larry Doyle Sr. and Mrs. Larry Doyle—Larry Doyle reportedly spent twenty-eight years living with the couple, totally immersing himself in their lifestyle. A source close to the production reveals that Larry Doyle's portrayal of his parents is "uncanny. It's almost as if Larry Doyle is slowing *becoming* his father—and his mother, too."

And finally, in what is sure to be a source of much controversy, Larry Doyle plays his own romantic interest in *LATW: The Larry Doyle Story*.

"I auditioned more than eight hundred actresses for the role," Larry Doyle says, "and none of them had exactly what I needed." Larry Doyle will not reveal how the love scenes in *LATW: The Larry Doyle Story* were photographed. "But I can tell you this," he says. "They're very funny—and they're *hot*."

LATW: The Larry Doyle Story will be released simultaneously in 5,200 theaters and 20,000 Red Boxes immediately upon completion. For the special-edition DVD, Larry Doyle will provide a full-length track of himself laughing in the appropriate places.

FOR FURTHER INFORMATION OR TO HELP FINANCE THIS FILM, PLEASE CONTACT LARRY DOYLE AT (410) 664-2161. IF SOMEONE ELSE ANSWERS, SAY YOU HAVE A QUESTION ABOUT YOUR ACCOUNT.

So [*Flintstones* director Brian] Levant recruited what he
called an "all-star writing team"—TV buddies from shows
like *Family Ties, Night Court* and *Happy Days*. . . . Dubbed the
Flintstone Eight, the group wrote a new draft . . . but it still
wasn't good enough. Four more roundtable sessions
ensued, each of which was attended by new talent as well. . . .

"It flips me out that there were so many writers, and
on any other kind of movie it wouldn't have worked,"
says Dava Savel, the lone woman in her roundtable. Savel
doesn't know if anything she wrote made it onto the
screen. "I have no idea if I have one line in there," she says.

—Entertainment Weekly

Last of the Cro-Magnons

A screeching comes across the sky.

Stately, plump Fred Flintstone stood upon the 'saur's head,
bearing a boulder of granite, on which a bird perched, its eyes

crossed. An orange dressing gown, ungirdled, was sustained gently behind him by the mild Mesozoic air.

He held his shell aloft and intoned:

—Yabba dabba dooo!

Afoot and lighthearted, he took to the open road, healthy, free, the world before him, the long brown path before him leading back to Bedrock.

Fred repeating to himself, as he ran, the words of an old song:

Flintstones, meet the Flintstones,

Fred Flintstone never made a lot of money. His name was never in the tablets. He was not the finest cartoon character ever drawn. But he's a *Homo sapiens.*

They're the modern Stone Age family.

He is simply a human being, more or less.

From the town of Bedrock,

Stonecutter for the world, tool maker, stacker of meat, player with reptiles and the nation's cave dwellers, balmy, gritty, growling, city of big boulders, Bedrock.

They're a page right out of history.

It was the best of times, it was the first of times, it was the age of ice, it was the age of lava, it was the epoch of large sloping foreheads, it was the epoch of dictabirds and monkey traffic signals and woolly mammoth shower massages. All the modern inconveniences. He feels the wind on his ears, his heels hitting heavily on the gravel but with an effortless gathering out of a kind of sweet panic growing lighter and quicker and quieter, he runs. Ah: runs. Runs. Keep on truckin'. He outlives this day and comes safe home.

See Dino run. Run, Dino, run.

Let's ride with the family down the street,

Let us go then, Hominidae, with the drive-in spread out against the sky, side of piquant bronto ribs from the takeout.

Through the courtesy of Fred's two feet.

What makes Fred run? Wilma, light of his life, fire of his loincloth. His sin, his soul. Wil-ma. Standing with her legs apart, she reminds Fred of Wondrock Woman.

When you're with the Flintstones,

"Oh, Fred," Wilma said, "we could have such a damned good time together."

Have a yabba dabba doo time,

"Some fun!" Barney said.

A dabba doo time.

"Shut up, Barney," Flintstone said.

You'll have a gay old time.

Once again at midnight nearly, while Fred pondered weak and weary over many a quaint and chiseled tablet of prehistoric lore; while he nodded, nearly napping, suddenly there came a tapping, as of something gently scratching, scratching at the cavern door.

Someday maybe Fred will win the fight

Nothing's more determined than a cat of saber tooth—is there? Is there, baby?

And that cat will stay out for the night.

The door was slammed by a thrust of a claw, and then at last all was still. The house was locked, and he thought his stupid cook or the stupid maid must have locked the place up until he remembered the maid was a mastodon and the cook a wacky collection of labor-saurus devices. He pounded on the door, tried to force it with his shoulder; he shouted,

Willllll-maaaa!

And so he beat on, fists against the granite, borne back ceaselessly into the past.

An Open Letter to All Academy Members, Creative Artists, and Anyone Else Who Still Believes in Freedom of Expression

It is with great sadness that I take out full-page ads today in the *New York Times*, *USA Today,* and *Variety,* though I weep not for myself alone but for the entire film community, for all of show business, and for the billions who depend on it for entertainment free of morality and the pieties of self-appointed spokesmen for God.

I am Demetri Pinot, a name a few of you may recognize from my music-video work, in particular Mandingus's "(I Need a 'Ho' with a) Big Ho," which won an MTV music award last year for Best Rap/Hip-Hop based on a Negro Spiritual. Some may also know me as the writer-director of this past Valentine's Day weekend box office champ, *Dead Girls Don't Cry.* But to many of you, I am simply the "hellbound pottymouth" behind *christblood.*

christblood is my attempt to come to terms with the divine mystery of the Resurrection, and most certainly not "a zombie picture with Jesus as an undead killing machine," as Mr. William Donohue, president of the Catholic League, recently claimed on his program, *Donohue & Donahue at the Movies*. It is worth noting that Mr. Donohue based his review on an early test screening, before any of the effects were laid in, and yet chose to condemn *christblood* WITHOUT HAVING SEEN A SINGLE FOOT OF THE COMPLETED FILM. Had he viewed the final cut, with its 234 digital effects and Trent Reznor score, perhaps Mr. Donohue would have seen *christblood* for the devout piece of entertainment it is.

In *christblood,* the character Jesus returns from the dead with a vengeance, a mangod on a mission, using his divine superpowers to destroy the Roman soldiers who cast lots for his clothing—and that's just the beginning. Donahue says this is sacrilegious. But how? This is more or less the legend set forth in the Book of Revelation; I have simply combined it with the Resurrection story line for greater dramatic impact. And let's not forget, THE GOOD GUY WINS. (But not before facing off against the entire Roman Empire.) Donohue also found "stunningly blasphemous" the scene in which Jesus "squirts blood from his stigmata into Pontius Pilate's face, apparently melting it." Again, the final effect is more convincing, but more to the point: What I did was simply physicalize Jesus's spiritual powers, transubstantiate them, if you will, into the kind of state-of-the-art pyrotechnics that today's audiences can truly believe in. As for the "obscene" Mary Magdalene scene, Donohue neglected to mention that she has sex with the apostles, not Jesus, and when he comes upon their grief-driven orgy, he expresses his divine displeasure in no uncertain terms. And for what it's worth, this scene no longer even appears in the domestic release, having only been included as an exigency of the foreign market.

I would like to say, "SEE THE MOVIE FOR YOURSELF AND DECIDE," but of course that is now impossible. Donohue's campaign against *christblood* has gone far beyond his unprofessional review and well into slander, harassment, and restraint of trade. As a result of his one-man anti-*christblood* crusade, the House of Representatives has attached a formal condemnation of my film to the current appropriations bill, New York mayor Michael Bloomberg has banned it from being advertised on city buses, I have been excommunicated, and Bill Maher suddenly isn't returning my calls. In response, my distributor has pulled *christblood* from its Christmas release schedule, and will only screen the film in Los Angeles and Manhattan in a one-week Oscar™-qualifying run.

The Inquisitional reign of terror has not ended there. The premiere of my film at last week's Twin Cities Film Festival was ruined when the projectionist opened the film canisters only to find them filled with blood. I cannot prove this was the WORK OF RIGHT-WING RELIGIOUS ZEALOTS, but *somebody* must have done it, just as somebody bribed my female escort at that event to begin talking in the voice of my dead grandmother at a most inopportune time, pleading with me to destroy *christblood* and devote the rest of my life to prayer. Later the same night, this same somebody filled my hotel bedroom with thousands of frogs—frogs, lest there be any mistaking their origin, which had been professionally trained to croak in unison something vaguely approximating the word "repent."

There can be only one response to this. All artists of conscience, and particularly voting members of the Motion Picture

Academy of Arts and Sciences, must make a show of solidarity against censorship. And what better way than to nominate *christblood* for the Academy Award in the categories of Best Picture, Best Director (Demetri Pinot), Best Screenplay Adapted from Another Medium (Demetri Pinot), and Best Supporting Actress (Sasha Grey as Mary Magdalene). These nominations would send a strong signal to DONOHUE AND HIS MINIONS and perhaps keep *christblood* in theaters through the symbolically important Easter weekend.

As artists, or those who consume the work of artists, you must be concerned about who or what Donohue will choose to unleash his holy wrath on next. Before you sit down to create or enjoy your next work of challenging art, think of me, lying here covered in black, gurgling sores unseen in the medical literature, and say to yourself, "There but for the grace of God go I."

Many in showbiz don't have a clear understanding of the writers' demands or the reasoning behind these demands.

—Variety

Why We Strike

OUR BELIEFS

We are artists. We may not dress all cool like artists, or get chicks like artists, and none of us are starving, quite obviously, but Hollywood screenwriters are certainly artists, perhaps even *artistes*. Okay, maybe we're not cranking out endless *Mona Lisa*s, but what about this Damien Hirst guy with his preschool spin paintings and cows suspended in barbecue sauce? If that's art, then *Ten Deadly*

Whispers, debuting exclusively on DVD this week, is art with a capital *R* (*for strong sexuality and some graphic violence*).

We suffer for our art. Not in a showy *oh-I-live-in-a-tenement-and-turn-tricks-to-buy-paint-and-have-this-special-tuberculosis-only-artists-get* kind of way. But we suffer just the same. We slave over our screenplays, alone, staring into blank laptops, often blinded by pool glare. And we smoke *real* cigarettes.

We struggle. We slave collectively over our teleplays, surrounded by fat people, crowded into ancient bungalows cluttered with free candy and soda. We go through all this only to have to listen with a wan smile as some Jeffrey tells us what's wrong with it, letting his bathrobe fall open to reveal he has a carrot up his rectum.

We are not in this for the money. Management would have you believe that we all make $200,000 a year. That's funny. We wouldn't even *eat* something that cost $200,000, unless it was actually $200,000, drizzled with truffle oil, the way Silvio makes it. *Yum.* The exact amount we receive under this new contract is meaningless to us, as long as it's more. The only reason why we require payment at all is to support those little people we keep telling you about: the assistants, amanuenses, baristas, Rolfers, scarf carriers, sycophants, and erotic muses we need to create our art. Oh, and our babies. And our various charities.

We are not cogs in some machine. While many of today's blockbusters are written by that machine, we are not cogs in it, despite having originally written all of the dialogue and characters and plot that this machine endlessly recombines and maximizes. When a bitter cop with a shattered family and a monkey on his back flees a narco-terrorist's fireball while cracking that he's getting too old for this, *some writer wrote some parts of that, some time back.*

Nor are we trained chimps. The last decent show written by chimps was *Jojo's Poop Party,* which was largely improvised.

OUR DEMANDS

An end to the lying. Just kidding. We recognize that, without lying, Management would be unable to exhale and thus perish. However, we are asking for a manifold increase in White Lies about how we are brilliant geniuses and the like, and a corresponding decrease in Brown Lies, about where our money is or what might happen in the future.

A fair share of newfangled revenue. Management is currently offering us bupkes of the monies they are making off Internet sell-through, streaming, ringtones, webisodes, cellisodes, iPadiSodes, celebrity-narrated colonoscosodes, or the psychotic episodes they've been beaming into your brain, brought to you by Clozaril™. All we are asking is 2.5 percent of revenue, based on 40 percent of gross receipts, divided by zero, in bullion. We believe this is a fair formula, yet complicated enough for Management to continue to find ways to exercise their screwing rights.

More respect. We are demanding unbounded respect bordering on worship, but that's just our opening offer. We'll accept far, far less, or even a good-faith reduction in spittle.

Meaningful consultation. While we acknowledge Management's right to rape our material, pervert its meaning, and cravenly dilute it for commercial use, we demand to participate in this process. We would like to be on set, or contacted by iPhone if the director doesn't want us there, and simply be asked, "Is this okay?" We stipulate that our opinion, coming, as it does, from the creator of the material being dramatized, is meaningless, and that Management can walk away or hang up before we even answer the question, but it would be nice, for once, to be asked.

A renunciation of droit du seigneur. As it stands, studio executives, from chairman down to associate producer, have the right to deflower us on our wedding night, or any other night or time of day of their choosing. We believe this can be written into our contract without affecting a similar agreement they have with the Screen Actors Guild.

Adequate parking validation. We know Management is deliberately understickering our tickets, and we want it to stop.

An inmate climbs onto the roof of a county jail and refuses to get down until prison officials can name all the members of *The Brady Bunch*. When the officials are unable to name all the Bradys, the inmate surrenders anyway.

> —Mysterious news item I read or heard sometime in
> January 1991 and then mysteriously forgot where

The Bradys, it is becoming increasingly clear, are a
genuine touchstone for a whole generation. . . . I do know
a few things about them. . . . I know that one of the Brady
children's name was Cindy. . . .

—Mysteriously popular writer Bob Greene in
his syndicated column, also from January 1991

". . . basically we study and treat Tubal abuse and other
video-related disorders."

"A dryin'-out place for Tubefreeks? You mean . . .
Hector. . . ." And Zoyd remembered him humming that
Flintstone theme to calm himself down, and all those
"li'l'buddy"s, which as they both knew was what the
Skipper always liked to call Gilligan, raising possibilities
Zoyd didn't want to think about.

Dr. Deeply shrugged eloquently. "One of the most
intractable cases any of us has seen. He's already in
the literature. Known in our field as the Brady Buncher,
after his deep although not exclusive attachment to that
series."

"Oh, yeah, that was ol' Marcia, right, and then the
middle one's name was—" till Zoyd noticed the piercing
look he was getting.

"Maybe," said Dr. Deeply, "you should give us a call
anyway."

"I didt'n say I could remember *all* their names!" Zoyd
yelled after him . . .

—Mysterious author Thomas Pynchon,
in *Vineland*, published that February

t.V.

chapter one

*In which Zenith,
a metaphor,
gets out of
bed.*

t.V.

ZENITH REMOTECONTROL, to be soon all things going as planned this pulsatile young morning the newly Dr.'d Zenith Remotecontrol, Doctor of the Tube, though not Tube Doctor, a real vocation, awoke in a state of static frenzy, her lips emitting a Tune—

All of them had hair of gold,
like their mother,
the youngest one in curls.

Rubbing the nightstuff from her eyes, lying aback, Zenith cocked a smile and went for the second verse:

Here's a story
of a man named Brady,
Bringing up three young men of his own—

—and lost it. Zenith blinked, and in a swallow, sent a

franchise-sized Big Gulp of twelve-molar hydrochloric acid gur-
gitating down, bypassing her stomach and pylorusing straight
into her duoden da dum dum. Her panicreatic juices joined the
fray, and Zenith, ascending, heaved herself into the bathroom.
Pepto Beach!

At the kitchen nook, with the K-Tube all the way up in vol-
ume, brightness, contrast, and color, Zenith stirred heaping table-
spoons of creamy pink Protective Coating Action into her coffee
and tried to compose for herself. Start from the beginning, she
thought. And it will come.

It came—

Here's a story
of a lovely lady
bringing up three very lovely girls.
All of them had hair of gold,
like their mother,
the youngest one in curls.

Here's a story
of a man named Brady
who was busy with three boys of his own.
They were four men,
living all together,
but they were all alone.

"Yes—" Zenith slamming her *Flintstones* chugamug down
onto Alf, alien taking the form, just now, of a placemat. The rest
spilled out like twoallbeefpattiesspecialsaucelettucecheesepickles
onionsonasesameseedbun:tilltheonedaywhenthisladymetthis

fellaandtheyknewitwasmuchmorethanahunchthatthistroupe
wouldsomehowformafamilythat'sthewaytheyallbecamethebrady
bunch.

Yes! Cut to the chase! Beep! Beep!

chapter two

~

In which Zenith
getting into her
car, com-
mutes.

t.V.

ZENITH PILED into her Tweety Yellow '72 Special Edition
Volkswagen Love Bug, which she had on good authority had stunt-
doubled *Herbie Rides Again*, but now bearing license plates reading
MY MOTHER, modified with hood ornament in the form of the rabbit
ears from a '55 Philco, nonfunctional in the physical sense but which
Zenith felt spiritually filled the machine with Ghosts of the Golden
Age, her dissertation and a few TubeTapes to watch on the way.

Submerging onto the 101, Zenith grabbed a Tape at random
and plugged it into the dashboard. A click and a whirr and the
right half of her windshield, illegally custom silver-screened using
a process currently a matter of trade litigation, glowed dead green
then phosphoresced into projected phantasms, and then finally,
after a few seconds, into good-old purple black-and-white. Zenith
rapped her fingers at ten and two and sang along

Dah—

Da—

Da dada da dada

Da dada

Da dada

Da da dada dada dada da

Vwooop! *Boom!*

Dr. Zenith Remotecontrol. *Oh, Rob!* Zenith Remotecontrol, Tv.D. *Shut up, Mel!* The culmination of 42,600 hours of programming, with limited commercial breaks. *Where can I buy a bald-headed voodoo doll?* More than 352,000 violent acts depicted. *Buddy! Yecch!* Nearly 600,000 laffs, guffaws, chuckles, and snickers, all meticulously videologued. *Walnuts!* Not to mention the hours Little Zenith logged in front of the Tube, knowing even then that this was to be her life's work.

Moe, Larry, the Cheese!

"What the—?" stabbing at the eject button. The Tape spat out of the console and Zenith zoomed in on it, careful to at all times keep one hand on the wheel. This was not her tape. Could not be. Not with Rob and Laura and Larry and Curly. And she doubted it could have come from the Institute. No self-respecting vacudemic would have mixed these vidoeuvres. Unless it was some kind of a sick Couchpotato joke.

The Tape bore none of the usual TubeTape markings—time, date, channel, the signs, and symbols of the profession. Only, scratched into the black plastic above the save tab, saved, two lowercase letters: tv.

There wasn't much time to ponder what all this little might

mean, because at that moment Zenith zigzagged across three lanes of traffic, wigwagging more responsible and less responsive motorists off the road and onto their Final Destination, and it was only through serendipity rather than perspicacity that Zenith looked up just then, into the jagtoothed face of the angry motorist cruising at seventy-five mph, about fifteen feet ahead and to her right, in an '82 Black K car, the specific details being oh so clear because of the twelve-gauge he had aimed at her head. He chose for her some choice words preambly, giving Zenith the chance to duck before her windshield enfenestrated into many thousands of rounded nuggets of glass, but what difference did that make? She was already going over the side anyway through the guardrail and tumbling end over end over end again with a half twist her and Herbie twirling off into the Twilight Zone.

chapter three

*The Crying of the
Whole Sick
Brady
Crew*
t.V.

THE F.J. MUGGS INSTITUTE for Video Studies, a public-private joint venture of the Japanese Ministry of Efficiency and the La-Z-Boy people, jutted from the Southern Californian hillside like a crystal mother lode, 6.2 acres of mirrored-blue polyhedron that evoked, perhaps not coincidentally, Galvantica, the geological nemesis of Godzilla in one of his lesser-known features. The highly reflective Institute shone like a citadel on a hill, particularly brightly between the hours of 11 A.M. and 2 P.M., when it tended to start brushfires. For this reason the Institute employed its own squad of firefighters, who scurried about the complex in hooded blue lamé jumpsuits, fooshing clouds of CO_2 at anything that smoked, and who at this moment stood ready to extinguish the heaving, steaming car wreck that poly-rolled into the parking lot with Zenith, at the wheel, still marveling at the airworthiness of these German automobiles.

"Oh, rilly! I shall be too late," Zenith declared, tumbling out of the Volk and grabbing up her entire academic career, with then a mad dash through the doors of the Institute, blood trickling down her left temple and her big hair festooned with beads of tinted glass.

By the time Zenith arrived, or rather landed, on the stage of the Institute's 950-seat $24 million Viditorium, there sitting in the front row already and bored, idly flipping through the Soaps on the Big Screen, was a jury of her peers.

- Victor La Mastersvoice, Acting Director of the Institute, who had made his reputation in the late '70s by delineating the Gilligan Paradox, positing that the reason the castaways did not simply kill the eponymous Gilligan was because even though the hapless sailor constantly bungled their attempts to escape the island, his survival was a sufficient and necessary condition for the continued existence of said isle, and thus their own continued survival.

- Bud Couchpotato, a rising star at the Institute, and some-
  one with whom Zenith shared a kind of David-Maddie
  sexual tension/intense hatred, both on-campus and off.
  Couchpotato was currently experimenting with transfer-
  ring film to video and back to film again, repeatedly, for
  reasons he had yet to make clear.

- Hanna Barbara DePatie-Freleng-Merrymelodies, a forty-
  something woman who Zenith secretly suspected was her
  mother, on the basis of peripheral glimpses she had caught
  of her during commercial breaks throughout her child-
  hood.

- And, finally, Quasar Qualitygoesinbeforethenamegoeson,
  who, though nearly 50 in this 18–34 game, had managed
  to maintain his sharpness and contrast. It was he who
  had successfully cracked the Minimum-Comedies Situ-
  ation (a perplex on a par with the Four-Color Theorem in
  mathematics), proving that all situation comedies could
  be deconstructed into five basic plots, rather than the six
  previously believed the minimum.

"Yer late!" La Mastersvoice barked, hitting the mute button
to command Zenith's full attention. "We were rilly hoping to wrap
this up in time for *Jeopardy!*"

"I know I'm rilly rilly sorry," Zenith replied, shaking her head
and knocking bits of windshield loose. "But, like, I was shot at on
the freeway and I—"

"You should make allowances for that kinda thing," inter-
rupted La Mastersvoice. "Now, let's just have it, huh?"

"Yes, yes, yes, um—" Zenith said, trying to regain her vertical hold. "I'm like rilly honored—" said Zenith, bowling over the stage to let him have it, her dissertation and a shower of shatterglass.

"Yeh—" gruff La Mastersvoice, with the old academic brush-off and a shove of Zenith's dissertation into the state-of-the-art vidsystem, which blipped the Big Screen then into the big bright face of Zenith Remotecontrol, looking considerably more poised and sheveled than she did just now, saying "I'm, like, rilly honored . . ."

Zenith sat beside herself, small hot and big cool, the hot bothered for she suspected her thesis, while high-concept, was not a this-crowd pleaser. Zenith's thesis was this, that:

People watch way too much TV these days.

Heavy, talking-heady stuff, especially difficult to dissert in a fifteen-minute video, fersure, and yet a supposition Zenith hoped would as hosted by PBS's Bill Moyers make low-calorie high-fiber good television. But the glazed look of the four in the front row told Zenith she was not yet mediuming her message.

And then, to her further horror, La Mastersvoice raised his arm and, taking jaded aim at her dissertation, pushed the fast-forward button.

Eight years of study swirled by like a badly edited Emmy retrospective, La Mastersvoice slowing it only once, for a classic scene in which Beaver and Whitey discuss the old new math, chuckling, and then zapped Zenith's academic career to an end.

In the deep dead air following, Zenith, going over her employment options, which were zip, stood awaiting the final credits.

After what seemed like miniseries, La Mastersvoice was heard: "Not bad. Coulda used more clips, but not bad atall."

Zenith felt renewed, picked up for a full season, as La Mastersvoice looked casually left and right, and went on: "An'body else got anything to say?"

"I have a question," a familiar voice descended from the dark back of the Viditorium.

Zenith squinted to make out the tall figure now dissolv—*omigod!*

It was a blast from her immediate past: the man on the freeway, still carrying the shotgun, which was the tipoff. But Zenith's gasp was accompanied by at least three others.

"Great Caesar's ghost!" said Qualitygoesinbeforethenamegoeson.

"T.V. Pychor!" bellowed La Mastersvoice.

"t.v.," whispered Merrymelodies.

It was, in a sense, all three: Dr. T.V. Pychor, founder of the Institute and in fact the entire Telegenic Movement, the High Priest of Low Culture, the man about whom NBC's Marshall McLuhan had said "T.V. *is* TV!," the current academic world-record holder of longest sabbatical at seventeen years so far, additionally the one-time mentor and lover of a young graduate student named Hanna Barbara, and moreover—

"I have a question," Pychor repeated. "Zenith, could you please name the Brady Bunch, in chronological order?"

"Greg, Marcia, Peter, Jan, Bobby, Cindy" came out of Zenith's mouth before she could think.

"And now, in order of popularity, based on fan mail, average per week?"

"Greg, Jan,"—again, Zenith speaking before it occurred to her that "—*daddy?*"

"Hey there, Opie Dopie," Pychor replied softly. "I came by to apologize for taking a shot at you on the freeway back there."

But this bit of epiphany went entirely unnoticed by the others, spitting as they were out questions or fragments thereof as they scrappled up the aisle, bowing down before the Father of Videotics:

Where have you what have you been doing watching taping all my wonder years latenight with large ensemble dramedy Bochco primetime soap Tabloid TV declining network-shares and furthermore MTV heavy or lite Bud Melman? until all the questions trailed off into the expectant faces of five, now joined by Zenith: global-village elders gathered around their T.V. Pychor.

"Wish I could help you," Pychor beamed back, "but my old thirteen-inch black-and-white blew out in '86, so right now I'm into this Ginny Woolf thing—who, as Cyril Connolly says, can spin those cocoons of language out of, like, nothing."

All together now their jaws dropped *bwoing!* to the floor in homage to the zanier alltoo infrequently broadcast Tex Avery cartoons.

Bliss

We Request the Honor of Your Presence
at GywnnandDaveShareTheirJoy.com

You have reached Gwynn Paley and Dave Maguire's Official Nuptials site. To continue, enter the GUEST ID and PASSWORD you received with your Wedding e-vitation. Please enjoy this short ad while the site loads.

Two blushing brides,
one rich, one poor,
both have their hearts set
on getting married at

the same romantic location.
On the same day.
Reese Witherspoon. Jennifer Lopez.
In love and at war
for:
The Wedding Pagoda
Opening June 14

Friends and Family (Who We Also Consider Friends)! I can't tell you how excited Dave and I are that you'll be able to join us as we Pledge our Love for years to come! Below you'll find all the info you need to help us make this Occasion as Special and Perfect as we have planned.

GUEST POLICY

E-vites are for the Guest only; there is no "implied plus-one." We're sorry, but it's a <u>very small mountaintop</u>, with limited ruins. We have gone to exhaustive lengths to achieve a proper mix of personalities, races, classes, ages, and orientations to ensure a Fun and Romantic Event for everybody. So don't be at all surprised to find that your True Plus-One is already there! (Though just one plus-one per guest, please; do you hear me, Erika?)

We regret, too, the no-children rule. Some of us feel that Children bring nothing but Joy to all occasions; others feel differently, and this is a discussion we've agreed to table until a later time. (Not *too* much later! *Tick tick tick . . .*) If it's any consolation, you'll be sparing your Little Loved Ones many <u>painful inoculations</u>, and then there's the whole <u>child-slavery</u> thing.

DIRECTIONS

Upon arriving at the Aeropuerto Internacional Jorge Chávez, in Lima, look for the Aero Sendero Terminal. It's a corrugated-metal shed, painted orange and possibly brown. Sendero, your pilot, should be there (he looks just like Erik Estrada, had things not gone so well for him). His Piper Apache is completely airworthy, and if it comes to that, somewhat seaworthy. After my father conducts a quick sobriety check, Sendero will wing you to a private airstrip on the shore of Lake Titicaca. From there, you'll travel via *balsa de tortoro,* or reed boat, to the island of Amantaní. The voyage is quite Authentic and will take about eight hours. Once ashore, llamas will take you up the mountainside of Pachatata (Father Earth), where you will be given a sleeping bag and assigned to a ruin.

A FEW TRAVEL TIPS:

- Do not let Sendero sell you any cocaine. We have made an exclusive arrangement with another supplier. Anybody wishing to partake of this indigenous fare *must* contact Dave's brother Drake. If you fail to do so, we may find ourselves short a best man.
- Lake Titicaca is a sacred Incan site. Their god or something rose out of it. Mocking its name, or the name of nearby Lake Poopó, is considered incredibly rude and has resulted in spontaneous stabbings.
- Since Pachatata is 13,615 feet above sea level, you may not be able to breathe. We will have oxygen on hand, but in limited supplies, so, unless you are absolutely certain you are going to die, please be considerate of others.
- If you look directly at your llama, it will spit in your eyes.

THE CEREMONY

You will awaken at 2 A.M. (it'll be too cold to sleep anyway) and llama it down <u>Pachatata</u> and then up <u>Pachamama</u> (Earth Mother). We should arrive at the peak between 4:30 and 5:30 A.M., depending on bandits, in time to witness the first light of the <u>Solstice</u>, at 5:58. The Incas believe if you stare into the sun as it rises on this day, you will be Reawakened to the Ancient Knowledge and Wisdom of the Cosmos. Hopefully, this will distract you from the sound of the seven llamas being slaughtered. (Some of you will have to walk back. Sorry.) Following a brief sacrifice to the Dragon Fertility Goddess (don't tell Dave!), we will enjoy a traditional breakfast of cooked potatoes and *mate de coca*, which is basically boiled cocaine and which I'm told puts Starbucks to shame.

The ceremony will take place at High Noon, officiated by a <u>Genuine Quechua Shaman</u> and, at the insistence of Dave's mom, Father Mulcahy, who has promised to keep his pagan comments to a minimum. First Shaman Klaatu will ritually purify the bride and groom (good luck with that!), followed by some <u>Catholic Mumbo-Jumbo</u>, and then we will exchange <u>Personalized Vows</u> written by me with input from Dave. In Andean tradition, the marriage will be sealed with <u>an exchange of shoes</u> (Luv those Incas!).

Two requests:

- In honor of the <u>Emperial Kantuta</u>, the sacred flower of the Incas, the bridesmaids will be dressed in tomato sateen, with the groomsmen wearing lemon velvet. Please avoid these color/fabric combos in your own ensembles.

- Our Ceremony was designed as a Spiritual and Romantic Once-in-a-Lifetime Chance for Heartfelt Reflection, and not as an opportunity to crack up Dave.

THE RECEPTION

The reception is scheduled for 4 P.M., or whenever the llamas are done. We ask that after the ceremony you gather as much firewood and wild potatoes as you can. In lieu of champagne, we will be serving chicha, made by the island's women, who chew up corn and other things and spit it into an earthenware pot for fermenting. It takes a little getting used to, but consumed in vast quantities, as is the tradition, it can sneak up on you. Accordingly, the Shaman will remain on hand to perform additional marriages as necessary.

Music will be provided by *¡Zamponas!,* a local pan-flute wedding band, playing Indigenous tunes as well as what sound like R&B hits from the '70s. Do not request the "Macarena" unless you want to hear a lot of screaming about *conquistadores sórdidos.*

Unfortunately, Dave and I will have to leave the reception early in order to make our plane to the Galápagos. And please: if anybody ties beer cans to the back of our getaway llama, I will cry.

ONE FINAL REQUEST

A lot of hard work and patience and tears and sexual compromise went into making this a Wonderful Celebration of Love. This is the wedding I've dreamt about ever since studying pre-Columbian civilization in the fifth grade. If you cannot enjoy and experience it appropriately, I ask that you to strongly consider staying home with the rest of Dave's buddies. (That doesn't apply to *you,* Dave!)

The Babyproofer

The baby doesn't like his flak jacket. It's Kevlar, the lightest material capable of stopping a large-caliber bullet, but it's awfully hot and it makes it hard for the little guy to sit up. Which is just as well, because *a sitting baby*, the babyproofer says, *is a sitting duck*.

We got our babyproofer through a friend, who came to visit after the baby was born and had a cow. *There are so many dead babies in this house,* she said, her fingers fluttering about. The wife got pretty upset, but this friend—really more my wife's friend—caressed her head, blotted her cheeks, and said the important thing was that our baby wasn't dead yet and there was still a chance we could stop the baby before he could kill himself.

The babyproofer cost seventy-five dollars an hour.

—*There's* a dead baby, he said, not a foot in the door, re: the staircase. Then, in a bouncing gesture along the baseboard: *dead baby, dead baby, dead baby . . . what is that?*

—What, that penny?

—Dead baby.

Our poor baby died so many times during that initial consultation: 187, according to the babyproofer's written assessment; it seemed like more. Dead baby in the toilet. Dead baby down the disposal. Dead baby with my scissors plunged into his carotid artery.

—Just curious, the babyproofer turned to me at one point. Did you *want* to have this baby?

The babyproofer needed a $10,000 retainer.

—For that kind of money, I said, just trying to lighten the mood a little, we could buy a whole new baby.

The wife did not laugh; the babyproofer stood up.

—I haven't lost a baby yet, he said. But who knows, maybe I am a little *overcautious*. Why don't you just buy one of those babyproofing books. They only cost about twenty bucks.

The babyproofer went through the initial ten grand rather quickly. In fairness, a lot of it was materials: 34 ceramic outlet guards @ $19.95 (the plastic ones, my wife agreed, weren't darling and they leached a substance that caused fatty tumors in cancerprone mice); 62 baby gates @ $39.95; 4 safes (pharmaceuticals, soaps and bath products; cleaning supplies; cooking and eating utensils; and assorted swallowables) @ $195. The Cuisinatal Food Reprocessor alone cost $3,000, but it does puree at twice the FDA's shockingly lax standards and can strain out some of your larger, harmful bacterias. There was some debate in our house as to whether we really needed 6 baby dummies (@ $699 per!), but I suppose the wife is right: if even one of them is stolen it's probably worth it.

Beyond the money, we've had to make a lot of adjustments, to create what the babyproofer calls a survival-friendly environment. Some of it makes sense, like not allowing anyone who has been to Africa, Southeast Asia, or Mexico into the house. But the hospital scrub-down before every diaper change seems excessive; it's so heart-wrenching, with the baby crying the whole time. And I do miss TV—though not enough to come home one day and find my lazy, violent, obese baby with a television set toppled on his head.

The thing I hated most was getting rid of the dog, but what could I do? It kept tasting the baby.

I haven't been sleeping much. I sit up in bed, worrying about all the money we've spent, but also whether we've spent enough. I go through each of the 187 dead babies in my head, running their fatal scenarios against the prophylactic measures we've taken. *Did I remember to spin the combination on the toilet?* I stare at the bedside monitor, waiting for the baby to flatline, which he does five or six times a night. So far it's just been that he's pulled off his wires again, but running in there five or six times a night and fumbling around for those shock paddles, it takes something out of you.

My wife and the babyproofer are driving up to Ojai, for a weekend seminar on antioxidant baby massage at some resort. I forget exactly why they can't take the baby; the spa supplies its own practice infants for insurance reasons, maybe.

So here I am, left holding the baby.

He is so beautiful. I want to lift the polarized visor of his helmet to get a better look; I want to kiss his cheeks, his nose, his forehead, damn the salmonella. But I can't. I know that. I rock the baby gently, in no more than a twenty-degree arc, no more than twenty oscillations per minute, whispering in the five-to-ten-decibel range, *Please don't die, baby. Please don't die. Not on my shift.*

Whacking the Baby

I want to kill the baby. These feelings are perfectly normal, I am told by Jimmy Ray DeHavre in *A Regular Guy's Guide to Rugrats*.

> He's monopolizing your wife's funbags, *your* funbags, sucking all the fun out of them (he's already plowed her love canal into the Chunnel); he's done something to your wife's brain, making her a baby slave with no time or inclination to service your needs; he's a crap factory, he's crying every goddam second, and you haven't slept in five days: of course you want to kill him. But don't. It's against the law. (p. 29)

My wife bought the book, though I doubt she has read it. There is much in it with which she would disagree.

I haven't slept in 234 days. According to www.askdrsam .com, I should be experiencing auditory and tactile hallucinations, severe motor and mental impairment, irritability, and death.

But, more likely, you *have* slept. Perhaps you have fallen into *micro-sleep* for periods lasting up to several seconds without noticing. Or perhaps you have fallen asleep and dreamt that you were awake and unable to fall asleep. Nevertheless, **sleep deprivation** can be a dangerous medical condition. If over-the-counter **sleep deprivation** drugs prove ineffective (to buy, click *here*), you should visit a doctor (to make an appointment, enter zip code and click *here*). If your problem persists, you may need to see a psychiatrist (click *here* for a live streaming therapy session). She or he will help you identify the source of your **sleep deprivation** and eliminate it.

She or he told me that every new father goes through this and that my suspicion that the baby is trying to kill me is unfounded and had I ever been institutionalized? Fifty dollars for fifteen minutes.

No point in confiding in the wife. She'll just take the baby's side again. There's definitely something going on between those two.

On day 246, I find myself in Little Italy, not knowing how I got there. I am standing in front of a building that I recognize from a *4news&more* report, the location of a social club reputedly frequented by alleged organized crime figures. I go in.

—I need someone whacked, I announce to no one in particular.

They seem entertained by my boldness. They let me up, and ask, who is it that I would like, how did I so colorfully put it, whacked?

—The baby.

I tell them I am not shitting them. They beat me up pretty bad. I walk into the apartment, a faceful of bad meat, and the wife says, quite concerned, I think the baby has an ear infection.

On the jacket of his book it says:

Jimmy Ray DeHarve has written several Regular Guy books, including *A Regular Guy's Booty Tips, A Regular Guy Wedding Planner,* and *A Regular Guy's Guide to Knocked-Up Wives.* He lives in Brooklyn with his wife and daughter.

Directory assistance says there's a James DeHarve on Carroll Street. I call and ask for Jimmy Ray and there is initially some confusion. Finally Jimmy Ray comes to the phone and I confide to him, regular guy to Regular Guy.

—Jesus fuck, he says, did you even *read* my book? Did you even read the next paragraph?

But trust me, the first time you're walking down the street and he tugs on your arm and says, "Hey, Dad, check out the rack on that one," you'll know it was all worthwhile.

I call Jimmy Ray back and tell him I can't wait that long; he hangs up on me, but not before advising me that only a "real scumbag" would even think about killing a baby.

It should be fairly easy finding a scumbag in New York City, you would think. I approach several groups of youths congregating on corners.

—I'm looking for a scumbag.

—Who you calling a scumbag?

Followed by some kind of a beating. Eventually, one fellow owns up to being a scumbag. We make arrangements. For an admitted scumbag, he has a very inflated view of his worth.

He is supposed to come on Tuesday night, but doesn't. I'm out a thousand bucks. Never trust a scumbag.

He comes on Wednesday night. I can hear him banging down the hallway. He'll wake the wife.

He'll kill the baby.

The scumbag has a knife.

The wife is downstairs, waiting to let the paramedics in. I am in the baby's room, pinching my gut, trying to form a tourniquet out of a fat roll. I should probably tell the police he was a black guy, or maybe that's racist. I wonder if they'll believe a Chinese guy. The baby wakes up and starts to cry. Great.

My wife won't like me getting blood all over the baby, but I pick him up anyway. Something about my warm, wet lap soothes him. He looks up at me, into me.

—*Dah-dah,* he says.

He puts a pacifier in his mouth and closes his eyes. I close mine. I'll get some sleep in the hospital, I think, and it's going to be all right.

The growth overtook Grover's mouth and he could no
longer eat. "Please," I begged my father. "He needs to go
to the doctor."

"Well, we'll see how he does," he said, waving me
away....

Grover died.

—From *A Wolf at the Table: A Memoir of My Father*,
by Augusten Burroughs

"That's not true," [Mr. Burroughs's mother] said, then
quickly corrected herself. "I should say we have different
memories."

—*New York Times*

She is writing her own memoir.

—Same article

Bad Dog

I'm not naïve. I knew the reviews might be bad, like that hatchet job in *Dog Fancy*. What I did not expect was to be sucker-punched by Oprah, or denounced from the floor of the U.S. Senate, or the mass crap-ins on my lawn. The price of truth, I guess.

I wrote *Tyrant Rex: His Life as My Dog* as a much needed corrective to *Speak: A Memoir,* and I stand behind my version, which costs three dollars less and contains many never-before-published candid photos of Rex.

His name *is* Rex, by the way, not Roo, or Rowr, or Bow Wow, or whatever it is he's calling himself these days. He's also mixed breed, not a rare Arubian Cunucu, or part dingo, as he has variously claimed. I know, because I raised him from a pup. I was the one who taught Rex to sit, to heel, to speak, and to speak English. His first word was not "out"—as much as that serves his current political agenda—it was "eat." I was there, and so was my chicken Parmesan. My therapist can confirm this.

I never struck Rex. If he now flinches at the sight of an open hand, he does so instinctually (or possibly for effect). I may have, on one or two occasions, rubbed his nose in something or other, but this was a widely accepted dog-rearing practice at the time.

Rex did, I'll admit, beg me to take him to the doctor to check out a "lump" that he found. But you have to understand, *he* begged for everything: for scraps, for ear scratches and tummy rubs, to go out at all hours of the night, to yet again rent *The Lion King*. He just barked all the way through. I would have happily taken him to the vet, if not for the simpering, and if not for the fact that we had been to the vet three times that month, twice for "anemia" that he attributed to a lack of "wet meat" in his diet, and once when he thought he was having a heart attack, which turned out to be the UPS guy. What Rex leaves out of his telling is that I did eventually take him to the vet, and the vet told him exactly what I had told him: the lump was his testicles. And let the record show that it was Rex himself who insisted that they be removed. Why would I force sterilization on a dog who could talk, if I am as greedy as his attorneys contend?

As Rex's fame grew with that ridiculous talk show (he scores an exclusive with Ahmadinejad and asks, "Do you own cats? You smell like cats"—please), his begging turned to growling. He barked and expected me to obey. He demanded wet meat, first cows by the carcass, then more exotic fare. He'd see something on the Discovery Channel and expect it in his bowl that very evening. He wanted to "taste all the animals," he told me, and once confessed his desire to "eat the last of its kind."

The cats.

God forgive me. I procured the cats.

But Rex ate them. In all likelihood, he is still eating them.

Need I point out that there remains one animal he has not yet tasted? (To my knowledge.)

Around the time he won the Peabody, the biting began. First, little nips at my heels for motivation; later, vicious bites on the calves and buttocks. (He was always careful not to break the skin.) One morning, I awoke to find him on my pillow, jaws agape, his fangs resting on my throat. He stood, licked my Adam's apple, and trotted away without saying a word.

The success attracted fleas: Rex lost himself in a cloud of sycophants and agents. He was doing a tremendous amount of catnip, even though it had no pharmacological effect on him. I pleaded with Rex, "Quit the show—we can make ends meet with the occasional corporate gig and go back to being what we are: a master and his dog." The next afternoon, I'm sitting backstage when one of Rex's pack sidles up to me and whispers, "Rex doesn't want you hanging with us anymore." Just like that. Rex could have told me himself. But he sends *Danny Bonaduce.*

The revisionist memoir was inevitable, I see now. Rex's true, loving upbringing didn't jibe with the Rex myth. Still, it hurt. I couldn't go into a Starbucks without his eyes piercing me from seven thousand counter displays, accusing me of unspeakable crimes against Canidae. I chose to remain above it, until I read that *Speak* was being made into a movie, with the part of me being played by Danny DeVito.

My reaction has, I believe, been measured and meticulously documented. If anybody is interested, my book can be purchased directly from www.tyrantrex.com. I will have nothing more to say publicly, except to extend my hand and issue one final, heartfelt command: Rex, come home.

Rü responds: It saddens me that Mr. Doyle has chosen such a public forum to discuss what is, despite my celebrity, a private matter. Clearly, we have different memories of my owned years. Pending litigation prevents me from commenting further. But I would like to add that while I can no longer call Mr. Doyle my master, and in spite of everything, I consider him my best friend.

I'm going to do a lot of fishing.

—Ed Nabors, co-winner of a $390 Mega Millions jackpot

What Am I Going to Do with My Mega Millions?

Good question. Here's a hundred dollars.

The truth is, I haven't really thought about it. I mean, I suppose I'll have to hire a lawyer to start preemptively suing people who claim I owe them money or fathered them or blinded them in a bar fight. And I'll need bodyguards with double-0 clearance, for insurance purposes. And another lawyer to sue the first lawyer. But beyond that, my life is going to stay pretty much the way it is, only with the Mega Millions.

Cheryl has been a good wife, financially supporting me all

these years while I pursued my dream of winning Mega Millions, and I'd like to keep her. She's not really a Mega Millionaire's wife, though, as she would be the first to admit. But in light of all her years of loyal service, I'm going to give her first crack at the position.

Out of my own pocket I'm advancing Cheryl up to $300,000 for a series of upgrades. She has all sorts of complaints about her face that frankly I don't see, but fine, we'll fix all that stuff. We'll also be installing state-of-the-art breasts, right above the original ones, which we'll keep around for old times' sake to remind us where we came from. To go with her new Mega Millions looks, Cheryl will be getting extensive training on trophy-wiving from Melania Trump, on loan from my new friend Don, at a special discounted rate.

I do hope it all works out, because Cheryl was with me back when it all started. All those scratch-offs. All that black stuff all over the bed. She's probably wishing she hadn't bitched so much about it now.

As for myself, I can't think of anything I want. Hair, maybe. Specifically, George Clooney's. So far he's been unwilling to part with it at any price, but we'll see how he feels about playing Khrushchev or Gorbachev or Blofeld or Mr. Clean in the new movie I'm financing. Plus he travels a lot, often to countries where it's possible to get what you want done done. You know what—that was off the record. Oh, and I forgot: here's a thousand dollars for each of you.

Also, I may get a heart transplant, just as a precaution.

We're going to keep the old house. We love the neighborhood, and we'll love it even more without a lot of the neighbors. We'll probably do some additions, preserving the original house as a centerpiece in the new living room, or maybe as a playhouse for all those grandkids we will no longer be denied. Cheryl's going to be too busy pleasing me to keep a house that large, so we'll need some kind of staff: just a few French maids, one of those sinewy masseuses with Chinese tattoos, some house lawyers, a night masseuse, and a butler. A really good butler, from England.

Out back I'd love to put in a small lake, where Tim Herlihy's place is now. We'll dock the yacht there, and copter it to whichever coast, as necessary. I haven't decided what to stock the lake with, but I've been thinking a lot about the environment now that I'll be owning so much of it. And it seems to me that the "greenest" thing to do would be get a bunch of those *Sports Illustrated* swimsuit models, brush some scales on them with biodegradable body paint, strap them in helmets rigged with a giant eyehook or an industrial-strength magnet on top, and toss them in. Maybe. Like I said, I haven't given it much thought. But I guess the short answer to your question is: I'm going to do a lot of fishing.

Acceptance

Please Read Before Suing

Dr. Goodbody's Total Goodbody System™ is such a revolutionary and completely natural way to eliminate all your health problems that it is quite common for people to feel frightened before using it and to feel disoriented and more frightened afterward. Before calling our customer-service line or 911, we suggest you sit down, drink eight glasses of water, and read our responses to the following testimonials, submitted by other satisfied customers just like yourself.

$750 FOR A 30-DAY SUPPLY? THAT'S $25 A PILL. ISN'T THAT A LOT OF MONEY?

—J. LOWELL, CHARLOTTESVILLE, VA

Not when you consider that that comes to just about a dollar an hour—a dollar for an hour free of all your pains and complaints. Wouldn't you pay a dollar to feel like a million bucks? You'd have to be crazy not to.

And it's not merely a "pill." Each Dr. Goodbody's Total Goodbody System™ daily bolus contains the entire line of Dr. Goodbody Solutions™, including ColoRooter™, BloodFlush™, TumorStopper™, and several others that are no longer available in most states. That's why each pill weighs nearly three ounces, and why we recommend you take it with eight glasses of water and the supplied lubricant.

MY DOCTOR HAS STRONGLY WARNED ME AGAINST
TRYING YOUR SYSTEM, AND TOLD ME NOT TO COME
CRYING TO HIM WHEN MY INSIDES FALL OUT.
                                    —C. MAZIN, BROOKLYN, NY

Of course your doctor would say that.

I HAVE BEEN TAKING MY DAILY BOLUS WITH EIGHT
GLASSES OF WATER FOR THREE WEEKS NOW AND HAVE
SEEN NONE OF THE RESULTS GRAPHICALLY DEPICTED
ON YOUR WEBSITE. INSTEAD I HAVE GAINED SIXTY
POUNDS AND HAVE BECOME SO BLOATED I NO LONGER
HAVE FINGERPRINTS. WHAT AM I DOING WRONG?
                            —T. O'DONNELL, SHERMAN OAKS, CA

You need to increase the size of the glasses of water. But keep the total number of glasses to eight.

I SMELL BURNING HAIR.

—D. MEYER, MADISON, WI

That means it's working. Other evidence that Dr. Good-body's Total Goodbody System™ is detoxicleansing™, immuno-blasting™, and revita-loosing™ your insides includes: headaches, nausea, vomiting, vomiting from places other than your mouth, tiny voices, rapidly cycling hypo- and hypertension resulting in staggering about with protruding eyeballs, cacophonous bowel sounds, muscle and joint pain that feels like slow roasting, inability to urinate, inability to cease urinating, spicy urine, sudden double-jointedness, itching in an unreachable location, cotton-mouth mouth, athlete's face, knee sap, extremely offensive odor that smells like strawberries to you, undead feeling, migrating love handles, reverse vertigo, cravings for bees and other sweet insects, Jolie lips, jazz hands, visible bubbles in blood, eye hair, abdominal rash that spells "LET ME OUT," uncontrollable urge to contact attorneys, unexplained French tips, laughing buttocks, and a blinding but oddly comforting white light.

If the burning-hair smell continues for more than a day, and your hair is not actually burning (which happens in only a small number of cases), there is a very slight possibility that you are having a stroke. If so, please seek help immediately by going online and ordering Dr. Goodbody's BrainReboot™. Choose overnight shipping.

I THINK I JUST PASSED MY SPINE.

—J. TURMAN, BANGOR, ME

That was your old spine. Rest assured that Dr. Goodbody's all-natural nanobiotic healthnauts™ are busily constructing a new spine for you, with fresh disks and state-of-art wiring. We think you're going to like it a lot. Do not be alarmed if, at first, your new spine feels somewhat gelatinous. This is a great time to try out all those frustrating yoga positions!

NO ONE IS ANSWERING THE GUARANTEED MONEY-BACK HOTLINE.

—M. GILVARY, LANCASTER, CA

All our operators are busy taking testimonials from other satisfied customers like yourself. Or they may be in the bathroom. We recommend that you take eight glasses of water and stay on the line, for as long as you can.

Cigarette Brands Targeting Specialty Niches in an Increasingly Challenging Marketplace

Chocoret Thins

A smooth chocolate taste in a tapered feminine design for women thirty-five and up. Comes in dark, light, or Chocoret menthol. Also available as an ice cream.

Liberty

For white men with some high school and a recent interest in political activism, Liberty exceeds all federal standards for tar and nicotine, and has been shown to cause cancer even in dead mice. "It's my right to smoke. It's my pleasure to smoke Liberty."

Midnight

An affordable cigarette targeted at runaways living in big cities. "For young punks who don't care what they put in their mouths."

iPuf

A social-networking app for pre-legal smokers, allowing them to virtually bum cybercigs from their friends and accumulate sophistication creds that can be redeemed for real smokes at age sixteen or if the clerk is cool.

Hound

The first cigarette designed specifically for canines. "All that bad doggy taste without that bad doggy breath."

I'm Afraid I Have Some Bad News

You might want to sit down. I wouldn't sit like that. You're going develop a real nice case of lumbosacral strain, and it's going to hurt for the rest of your life. You'll end up going to a chiropractor twice a week for the next sixteen years, and every time you go he's going to ask you if you've been doing your exercises and you're going to admit that you lost the sheet, and he's going to give you another sheet and charge you a hundred bucks. Meanwhile, the pain will be getting worse and you won't feel like having sex anymore and your husband is going to start looking around, and who could blame him, you've gone from being a reasonably attractive wife to a whiny sack of no sex.

Your husband? I'll get to him.

So he's out there, banging some prostitute (not wanting to start a relationship, out of respect for you), completely unaware he's being filmed for an HBO documentary. Of course, he catches this new hepatitis G, which makes hepatitis C look like hepatitis A, and which also makes your kidneys explode, possibly harming innocent bystanders. You, in turn, are going to take up with your chiropractor, the only man still willing to touch you, and that's going to get expensive.

So if I were you, I'd sit up straight.

Anyway, your husband has what we call a "medical condition." Without getting too technical, I should warn you this next part is going to make me look smart and you feel stupid, and it's also pretty gory.

Your husband was admitted with extreme pain in the abdomen, which is obviously not our fault. Now, pain in the abdomen can be caused by any number of things, from comical food poisoning, which strikes in the middle of a fancy dinner party, to fatal— or *non*comical—food poisoning, to a three-hundred-pound tumor composed of hair and teeth, possibly the overgrown unborn twin his mother mourned instead of ever loving him.

We didn't want to rule anything out, so we opened him up.

There were no multi-hundred-pound tumors; that's the good news.

However, it's a real mess in there. There's a lot of intestinal tubing squishing around—what you call "guts"—as well as an assortment of small, esoteric organs they don't spend a lot of time on in medical school. And bear in mind that everything's pretty much the same color, not like in the textbooks.

After securing the kidneys as a precaution, I took a step back and opened the floor to suggestions. This is a teaching hospital, so there's always a bunch of smartass interns wandering around thinking they know everything. The "diagnoses" put forth—crazy, scary stuff—were summarily dismissed, because God forbid one of these snot-nosed wanna-docs is right.

I did a little preliminary exploratory surgery, employing what is known as the "scream test," which involves poking various organs and seeing if the patient screams. That usually indicates a problem. The procedure is trickier when the patient is sedated, of course, but I've been known to get a decent scream out of patients who were technically dead. So I did some poking and prodding, but then I remembered I had an eye appointment, so I decided to close him up. And that's when . . . well, you might want to stand up and sit back down again. I don't know why; I find it helps, and I'm the doctor.

First, the good news. Your husband's portfolio looks great; I can't believe he got into Apple at twelve—pre-split twelve. I'd say the prognosis for your long-term financial health is excellent. However, last month your husband dumped seventy-eight thousand dollars worth of Clo-Pet, the pet-cloning outfit, two days before it was revealed that Dr. Kalabi was not in fact cloning clients' beloved companions but instead creating look-alikes, using plastic surgery and transplanting pieces from other pets. Yesterday, the SEC and IRS swooped in and froze all your husband's accounts— which may explain his abdominal pain—and then, talk about bad luck, this morning the CEO of your health-insurance carrier fled to Argentina with a transgendered dominatrix, owing me literally millions of dollars.

So, unless you've got fourteen thousand dollars in cash or a certified check, I'm going to have to leave Douglas wide open on the table. And it's very cold in there.

Excuse me? He's not your husband? Then whose—

Goddamn it. I'm going to have to go through that whole thing again. Great. Okay, well, then, who *is* your husband?

Oh.

I'm afraid I have some very bad news.

Breakfast Updates

Eating breakfast now. Yum!

(thelarrydoyle via Tweetdeck)

Man, bacon is delicious!

(thelarrydoyle via Tweetdeck)

I could eat bacon all d

(thelarrydoyle via Tweetdeck)

Life is an improvisation.

—Annoying saying

Eulogy for Bob

A Wake. Musical director ROZ *plays somber organ music offstage right.* FATHER O'DOULE *stands at a podium located center stage, directly in front of the tabernacle. Stage left is an open casket, bearing* BOB HARTWICK. *He is deceased.*

FATHER O'DOULE: Bob Hartwick was a gentle man. He was a kind man. He was a funny, funny man. But above all, he was a courageous man. At the age of forty-four, when most men would have accepted their lot in life, Bob Hartwick quit his job as creative director at Leo Burnett Worldwide, liquidated his assets, and divorced his wife in order to pursue his lifelong dream: to start his own improvisational comedy troupe. And while the Giggle Gas Factory never hit it big, exactly, they were getting more and more out-of-town bookings, and their most recent revue, *I Hate This Damn Job, But I Can't Seem to Stop Laughing,* had gotten some very encouraging reviews. In fact, it is a testament to Bob Hartwick's improvisational ability that last Thursday night, when he suffered a massive heart attack during the "Larry King and I" sketch, the audience laughed for a full six minutes before realizing it was not a put-on. It is perhaps sadly ironic that, had Bob received appropriate medical attention more quickly, he might still be with us today. But those who knew Bob Hartwick know he would have wanted to go out on a laugh. As you can probably guess, the Giggle Gas Factory was everything to Bob Hartwick. Consequently, I have asked a few people who knew Bob best, his fellow Giggle Gas Factory workers, to say a few words.

O'DOULE *exits to vestibule upstage left and the surviving* GIGGLE GASSERS—DESMOND, HELEN, CATE, *and* JEFF—*trot up to the altar. They are in mourning: black jeans and gym shoes; black T-shirts with a reversed-out Giggle Gas logo.*

DESMOND (*reflexively cheerful*): Thank you, and good afternoon everybody! (*Failing to get enthusiastic response, he suddenly realizes* BOB HARTWICK *is dead. He is crestfallen.*) But seriously, let's not kid ourselves: Bob Hartwick *was* the Giggle Gas Factory. He was our foreman, but also our coworker; he was the man who turned on the Giggle Gas. And now, with his passing, that gas has been reduced to a slow leak. Bob Hartwick, quite simply, was irreplaceable.

HELEN (*cutting in perkily*): But we *are* taking applications!

DESMOND (*laughing good-naturedly*): You know, we make jokes; but that's what Bob Hartwick's life was all about: making jokes, making *you* giggle. And in honor of that, we wanted to give Bob the sort of eulogy we'd like to think he would have liked to have given himself.

JEFF (*to* MOURNERS): But first, we need an occupation. A normal everyday occupation.

MOURNER ONE: Gynecologist!

MOURNER TWO (*drunkenly*): Proctologist!

HELEN *and* CATE *put their hands on their hips in mock disapproval.*

DESMOND (*in his deep* ANNOUNCER *voice*): Please. Remember, this *is* a funeral.

MOURNER THREE: Mortician!

JEFF: We already have one of those.

MOURNER FOUR: Television anchorman!

JEFF: All right, television anchorman.

CATE (*as* HARRIET LEGGS, *her strident feminist character*): Or anchor*woman.*

DESMOND: Yes, of course. This *is* the new millennium. Now, what we need is a last line, or I suppose in this case (*chuckling*), we should say *last words.*

MOURNER ONE: Good-bye, cruel world!

DESMOND (*in his deep* GAME SHOW HOST *voice*): And remember, originality counts!

MOURNER THREE: AAAaargh!

HELEN (*pointing to* MOURNER THREE): I'm sorry, we don't do double funerals!

ROZ provides rim shot.

DESMOND: All right, the occupation is television anchorman, or anchorwoman, and the last line is (*in uncanny impression of* MOURNER THREE) "AAAaargh!" (*aside to* MOURNER THREE) Is that with five *A*'s? (*listens to nonexistent response*) Aaaargh with four *A*'s. Well, then, without further ado (*in his* ED RALPHWARDS *voice*), Bob Hartwick, *this* is your eulogy!

CATE *and* JEFF *position themselves in front of the open casket.* CATE *assumes persona of* DEBORAH GUMBALL, WGAS-TV *anchorwoman. She stops* JEFF *as he walks by.* ROZ *provides the "Acting News" theme.*

CATE: Sir, sir, could you please tell us how you felt when you found out that Bob Hartwick had died?

JEFF (*horrorstruck*): What?! Bob Hartwick is dead?! (*dropping to his knees*) There wasn't anything about this in Arts & Leisure?!

DESMOND: FREEZE!

DESMOND *runs in and taps* JEFF *on the shoulder, drops to his knees, and quickly assumes* JEFF's *position.* DESMOND *then goes into his memorable* TATOOIE *character from the "Beyond the Return to Giggle Gas Island" sketch.*

DESMOND (*pointing to casket*): De corpse! De corpse! (*pause for laughter*) Boss, what is your Bob Hartwick fantasy?

CATE (*in her* RICARDA MOUNTEBANK *character*): Well, Tatooie— (*A beat.* DESMOND *wipes an imaginary goober from his eye.*). My fantasy is that Bob Hartwick could still be with us, bringing mirth and laughter to all of Giggle Gas Island. But failing that (*She walks over to caress the casket lining.*), my fantasy is to see Bob Hartwick laid out in reech Corinthian leather . . .

HELEN: FREEZE!

HELEN *runs in and taps* CATE *on the shoulder. She continues* CATE'*s gesture, cradling* BOB HARTWICK'*s lifeless head in her palm.*

HELEN (*dramatically*): Alas, poor Hartwick, I knew him, Tatooie. (*She wipes imaginary goober from* BOB HARTWICK'*s eye.*)

JEFF: FREEZE!

JEFF *runs in and taps* DESMOND *on the shoulder. From the kneeling position, he stands and begins to lurch toward the coffin.*

JEFF (*as* EEGORE, *the delightful pastiche he created for the "Haunted House on Pooh Corner" sketch*): Master, master. (*shuffling, deadpan*) I brought you that new brain you wanted. It's from the *Times* theater critic. It's never been used.

HELEN (*as* DR. POOH): Oh, bother, Eegore! (*Turning* BOB HART-

WICK's *face toward* MOURNERS) This was Mr. Bob Hartwick! He deserves better than that! Oh, bother!

CATE: FREEZE!

CATE *runs in and, as a joke, taps* BOB HARTWICK *on the shoulder, cracking* HELEN *up. She then assumes* HELEN's *position, as* THE FRIGID MORTICIAN *from the revue, "The Giggle Gas Chamber, or I Hereby Sentence You to Laugh Yourself to Death."*

CATE (*scolding* JEFF): How many times do I have to tell you? Face up! Face up! (*She uses* BOB HARTWICK *to illustrate*) Not to the right! Not to the left! Face up!

JEFF (*in his* SKEETER *voice*): Uhhhhhhhh, oh-kay.

DESMOND: FREEZE!

DESMOND *assumes* HELEN's *position, but in his own mortician character,* MORTY, YOUR DISCOUNT SARGOPHAGUS SALESMAN.

DESMOND (*with a stiff sweeping gesture*): Now this one's a very nice, very nice. Our Bob Hartwick model. A big seller.

JEFF (*comically hesitant*): But . . . uh . . . there's already a . . . a person in there.

DESMOND: It's a demo. I can knock fifteen percent off the list.

JEFF (*resting his hand inconspicuously on the side of the casket*): Well, I was thinking of something, uh, a little less, uh, *occupied.*

DESMOND (*annoyed*): The customer's always right, right? Right.

Here, I've got a very nice fiberglass item, if you'll walk this way....

Before JEFF *can respond "If I could walk that way, I wouldn't need the embalming fluid,"* DESMOND *flips the casket lid shut and it falls on* JEFF's *hand.*

JEFF: AAAARGH!

Recognition of these "last words" causes MOURNERS *to break into spontaneous applause. Over the applause,* JEFF, HELEN, DES-MOND, *and* CATE *stand in front of the casket, holding hands, and take a bow. As the applause continues, they stand back and gesture toward the coffin.* JEFF *opens the casket to once again reveal the body of* BOB HARTWICK, *prompting increased applause. The soul of* BOB HARTWICK *rises from his earthly remains and takes its place in line with the living* GIGGLE GASSERS. *Wild applause. The coffin lid drops on the spectral hand of* BOB HARTWICK. *The phantasm feigns great pain. Hysterical laughter.*

Fade to eternal black.

Rapture

Today fur.
Tomorrow leather.
Then wool.
Then meat ...

—An important message from
the Fur Information Council of America

Then What?

Then

they came and told me I had to free my dog. I still remember
what I said.

I said: *What?*

—It's immoral for one animal to hold dominion over another
animal, the taller one said.

—It's a form of slavery, the shorter one added.

—I see, I said, and I thanked them for their input and closed the door.

Then

when I opened the door again several minutes later, the taller one said: I'm afraid we're going to have to insist.

—Look, I said, I don't have all day to talk to kooks.

But then,

as it turned out, they weren't kooks.

As it turned out, they were the police. And, as it further turned out, there had been some elections a while back and a lot of those green people had been swept into office and had passed all sorts of legislation, the gist of which meant I had to free my dog.

—We don't write the laws, the taller one said. I have a dog myself. Had. Now we're just friends.

—But my dog likes it here, I said.

—Ahhhhhh, the shorter one said.

They had all the answers.

And, in any case, the Pet Emancipation Act (PEA) was fairly clear on the matter, particularly with regard to fines and minimum prison terms. And so I said good-bye to Charlie, my best beagle buddy of nearly ten years, and emancipated him.

Charlie spent his first hour of freedom visiting all the yards directly adjacent to ours, eating garbage and doing all his other favorite things to do outside, and then he came romping back home, scratching and whining at the door.

I let him back in, and some people jumped out of the bushes and

then

I was on my way downtown as part of a massive FBI sting operation. I ended up paying a $1,500 fine, and Charlie was given new tags and relocated to another state under the Federal Witness and Animal Protection Program (FWAPP).

I don't know what I expected to happen, I guess I thought that maybe old Charlie, braving the brute elements and traffic, would somehow find his way the hundreds and hundreds of miles back home. But beagles don't travel well. Charlie, or whatever it is he calls himself these days, was gone.

But then,

anyway, I had other things to worry about once I got home. The neighborhood was literally crawling with freshly freed pets: and not just dogs and cats and parakeets and tropical fish, but poisonous snakes and lizards and several varieties of rodents. And a lot of those little turtles they supposedly stopped importing years ago.

The tropical fish and birds and turtles didn't fare too well on the outside, and it wasn't pleasant to watch (more unpleasant, though, was the fact that no one was ever too sure what happened to the rodents and the rest of the reptiles). But the dogs seemed to adjust okay, quickly forming support groups of about eight to fifteen; and the cats managed to scrape by, if just barely. It appeared that everything was going to be just fine—that is, until the fish and birds and turtles ran out.

Then

the dogs went bad. Almost overnight, they succumbed to some kind of ugly mob mentality, and soon it was unsafe to leave the house without a twenty-five-pound bag of dog food;

and then,

not long after that, dog food was no longer good enough for them, and since there wasn't any meat anymore, the dogs became very difficult to please. The cats, in turn, became quite unsociable and began spending all of their time up in the trees, a vantage point from which they frequently would come hissing and clawing down onto your head, without provocation.

The police refused to do anything about any of this, saying their hands were tied by the Free Animals Are Not Subject to Human Laws Act (FAANSHLA). So things were pretty wild around my neighborhood, at least until that first winter.

Then,

the following spring, they came for my clothes. Under the Non-Exploitative and Environmentally Sound Use of Fabrics for Fashion Act (NEESUFFA) it became illegal to wear, or own, or assist in wearing, or try on, any garment, or draping, or accessory made in whole or in part from animals or animal by-products, petroleum products, or cotton harvested with a threshing device. They left me with a two-week supply of recycled-paper gowns and a phone number I could call to become a regular subscriber.

But then

the American garment industry sprang into action. Having already successfully circumvented U.S. labor laws, it had little trouble getting around this one. By June, the clothing stores were completely restocked with a wide selection of high-fashion outerwear made from technically nonexploitative and environmentally sound fabrics: corn-silk shirts, whole woven-wheat suits, rice pants, stoneground denims, and soy-T's.

This, then,

led the courts to rule that threshed-grain fabrics violated

the spirit if not the letter of NEESUFFA, and by August we were
back to wearing recycled-paper products and earthen shoes. Re-
tailers promised a full line of winter claywear by fall,

> but then

> it failed to pass constitutional muster.

Then

> Congress passed the All Animals Are Equal in Educational
and Employment Opportunities and Environmental Access Act
(AAAEEEOEAA), which mandated, among other things, the teach-
ing of nesting and male display in public schools,

> which then

> led to the formation of the Department of Animal Niche, Ter-
ritory, Habitat, Roost, and Coop Services (ANTHRCS), which was
responsible for finding safe and dignified housing for all animals,
except for humans, who were already served by the Department of
Housing and Urban Development (HUD) and which further led to
a landmark court case in which a pack of timber wolves used their
rights of eminent domain to force the relocation of five families in
northern Minnesota.

> Now then,

> all this has taken some getting used to. Free-range fruits
and vegetables are okay, I guess, if you get to them not too long
after they've hit the ground, but I do miss eggs and milk and
cooked food, and I know this will sound odd, but I miss the
chance to wash my clothes. And while I'll admit it is safer to walk
in the woods since they banned hunting, and it's much easier to
save money now that it's worthless, the fact is, you can't walk on
the grass anywhere anymore, and it's downright dangerous to go
to the zoo. So then,

I suppose if I had known
then
what I know now,
well then,
I guess I would have never signed that petition.

Court Under Roberts Is Most Conservative in Decades

—*New York Times*

Recent Supreme Court Decisions

The justices ruled 6–3 that "professional intuition" is sufficient cause to prompt a search of persons or property. The Court upheld the constitutionality of a "blanket search warrant" issued in 2010 by a federal judge in Texas authorizing the search of the residence or vehicle of "any persons answering to the names Angel, Enrique, Juan, Manuel, Pedro, Jesus, or Ramon."

By a 5–4 majority, the Court voted to further narrow *Roe v. Wade*, upholding an Idaho law granting women unrestricted access to abortion "except in those cases in which the woman is pregnant or the abortion will somehow impair her ability to become pregnant in the future."

Voting 7–2, the justices ruled that children under the age of eighteen have "only those rights conferred upon them by the state, or their parents." The case stemmed from a February 2009 incident in which the principal of an Austin, Texas, grade school conducted full body-cavity searches of twenty-seven third-graders in an attempt to locate a missing chalkboard eraser, which was never found.

Reversing California's high court, the justices voted 6–3 to reinstate the disorderly conduct and resisting arrest conviction of Laurence S. Williams, who was apprehended by the California Highway Patrol after "making voodoo eyes" at one of its officers. The decision was moot, however, as Williams was released following the state court's action and subsequently was shot and killed attempting to leave the scene of a double-parking incident.

Quick-fix artists are now in a frenzy over guns. But let's be honest and recognize that the overriding issue isn't really gun control.

    —Former vice president Dan Quayle, blaming school shootings on a lack of prayer in schools, a liberal legal system, and a popular culture "that transmits counterculture values"

Cherry Garcia, Wavy Gravy, Phish Food, Dave Matthew's Band Magic Brownies

    —Flavors of Ben & Jerry's Ice Cream that are sold to children and named for the late hippie singer, the hippie clown, the marijuana-loving hippie band, and marijuana-laced pastries, respectively

Freezer Madness

Damien Thorn needed a fix. He had had another hard day at William J. Bennett High School, where his more popular classmates had again teased him about his long hair, blue jeans, and out-of-step political views. Damien felt like screaming. For ice cream.

At 4:50 P.M., the impressionable sixteen-year-old entered the Piggly Wiggly supermarket in Heartland, a tightly knit midwestern community. He went straight for the grocer's frozen food section.

He stared down the endless, gleaming freezer, his young eyes glazing over. There were dozens of flavors to choose from, and no one to tell him that any one flavor was the "right" one. Vanilla, chocolate, strawberry? *Traditional* flavors, he sneered, for *squares*.

He pulled out a container. Bovine Divinity: *Milk chocolate ice cream and white fudge cows swirled with white chocolate ice cream and dark fudge cows.*

"Cows are gods," he chuckled. "Cool."

Damien peeled up the cover and plunged his finger deep into the intermarried chocolate and vanilla. He sucked his finger, savoring the creamy anti-Christian message. Almost immediately, he felt a tingling in his brain. He tossed the opened container back into the freezer, having no intention of paying for it.

He opened the next container: Brownie vs. the Board of Education. Delicious.

The sugar and fat were giving him a definite "buzz" now, and he began pawing through the cold metal shelves, promiscuously touching, tasting...

Karamel Marx, Lenin Meringue, Julius and Ethyl Rosenberry... *Next row, next row.*

Fudge Blackmun's Roe v. Walnuts, Godless Chocolate Cake, Morsel Relativism, Plumiscuity...

More, more, no limitations...

Greenpeach, Gum Control, Pro-Gay Agenda Swish, Creamy Sex Education in Schools with Free Condom Swirl . . .

Oh, sugar, sugar! Oh, honey, honey . . .

Up Against the Wall, Fluffernutters! The Revolution Will Not Be Caramelized! Chill Your Parents!

Damien sat in the middle of the aisle, splayed legs, frost-burned fingers, three dozen pints of immoral mess oozing around him. He grinned stuporously, his pupils ricocheting like Mexicans scurrying across the border.

Then he saw it.

He crawled into the case, clawing at the one remaining, ice-encrusted container. Still inside, he scraped the frost away with his thumbnail:

THE WORLD'S BEST VANILLA

"Vanilla ice cream made with pure vanilla extract." A laugh escaped and hung in the frozen air. So perfect, so pure. And heavy, he noticed. And hard.

At 7:53 the next morning, Chip White, the star quarterback of the WBHS Values, was standing at his locker, ministering to some members of the cheerleading squad, when he did not notice a wild-eyed Damien Thorn approach him from behind, raise above his head a blue cylinder with the now all-too-familiar psychedelic lettering, and *Hello, we're Ben and Jerry, and we really must protest at this point. We know what the author is trying to do here, and we don't like it one bit. To our knowledge, no Ben & Jerry's prepacked pint has ever been used in the commission of a first-degree murder. And, we cannot state more emphatically, we do not condone this use of our product. Also, and not to nitpick, but most of the flavors referenced above are not and never were available for sale in supermarkets, but only in our 350 franchise scoop shops across the country.*

As to the larger issue, let us reiterate that the link between premium ice cream and violence is tenuous at best. Millions of teen Americans enjoy our fresh, delicious ice cream regularly and do not go on rampages of any kind. Recent legislative efforts to place age limits on the consumption of Ben & Jerry's will, we believe, drive children to consume subpremium ice creams high in chemical preservatives and pumped full of air, as was common during the Vietnam War, with potentially tragic results.

At Ben & Jerry's, we make premium ice cream from only the finest natural ingredients and pure Vermont cream, and do not support the violent overthrow of the United States government at this time.

Some of Hollywood's top action filmmakers—men behind such octane-fueled thrillers as "Die Hard" and "Delta Force One"—are helping the U.S. Army dream up possible terrorist threats America might face in the future and how to handle them.

The counter-terrorism brainstorming sessions are the latest focus of the Institute for Creative Technologies, formed in 1999 at the University of Southern California to develop advanced training programs for the Army, institute officials said Tuesday.

"The group looking at counter-terrorism is really an extension of the kind of efforts we've been doing for about two years," one institute official said. "The benefit of the entertainment group is that they think more creatively. They think outside the box."

—Variety

Pop Corps

Brig. Gen. Alan Spangler presided. In attendance from the entertainment community were: Sandy Duckler, film producer (*Thrill Kill, The Last Jihad, The Fragging of Lieutenant Chapman, Where's the President?*); Hanna Amann, screenwriter (*Executive Privilege, Diplomatic Immunity, Breach of Protocol*); Joshua Patrick Stern, screenwriter (*My First Girl, Dennis the Menace IV: The Pubescence, Carnispore*); McBoog, commercial, music video, and film director (*Monkey Fist, Iron Toes, The Razor's Kiss*); Capri Sunset, television writer-producer (*Mutanauts, X-Mammals, Junior Mutanauts*). Sitting in the back were Mr. Turner and Mr. Cooper, button salesmen from Langley and Quantico, Va., respectively.

Gen. Spangler welcomed the participants and complimented them on their patriotism. He said this initial meeting was to be a "bull" or "brainstorming" session, that there were no right or wrong scenarios, and that everyone should feel free to pitch their edgiest stuff. Mr. Duckler asked, "Who do I have to [orally copulate with] to get a latte around here?"

After coffee was delivered, Gen. Spangler again solicited terrorist scenarios.

"What if," Mr. Stern began, "the bad guys got a hold of a small device, fits in the palm of your hand, which can knock out everything electronic—cars, planes, kidney machines—within a mile radius?"

"An electromagnetic pulse device?" Gen. Spangler asked.

"Right," Mr. Stern said. "I couldn't think of the name."

"Need to raise the stakes," Mr. Duckler said. "Make it a hundred miles."

"A mile is plenty," Gen. Spangler said. "And how would you power such a device?"

"I was thinking, some kind of ancient sacred ruby," Mr. Stern said.

"We did that on *Mutanauts*," Ms. Sunset said.

"I don't watch *Mutanauts*," Mr. Stern said. "I've never watched the show."

Gen. Spangler asked the participants to please move on.

"Just blue-skying." Ms. Amann suggested a scenario in which a "Black Muslim, angry but not unrelatable, meets a mysterious Arabic woman at an Islamic social function."

"Will Smith and Eva Mendes," Mr. Duckler suggested. Mr. Stern pointed out that Ms. Mendes is Cuban. Mr. Duckler felt that it was racist to think Ms. Mendes could not play other minorities. "Do they have to be Muslim?" wondered Mr. Stern. "That feels played out to me." Mr. Duckler thought that perhaps Ms. Mendes could play a radical lesbian separatist. That's what ruined Mr. Duckler's remake of *Casablanca*, Mr. Stern opined. Mr. Duckler then assessed Mr. Stern's professional credentials in disparaging and profane terms. Mr. Stern stood, and appeared to be about to climb across the conference table when he was subdued by two MPs and escorted from the room.

Gen. Spangler asked Ms. Amann to please continue with her scenario.

Mr. Smith's character falls hard for Ms. Mendes's, Ms. Amann explained, but then he begins to suspect she is a member of a rogue sect bent on bringing down the entire U.S. government.

"On Valentine's Day," Ms. Sunset proposed.

"Puts a clock on it *and* gives it heart," agreed Mr. Duckler. "*Sleepless in Seattle* meets *Jagged Edge* or *Basic Instinct,* or *Sliver* or *Jade*. I can deliver Eszterhas."

"He's dead," said Ms. Amann.

"He was a dear friend," said Mr. Duckler.

"Anyway," Ms. Amann continued, Mr. Smith's character

"must decide whether his love for this one-woman harem [Ms. Mendes] and his hatred of institutional racism ultimately outweigh his patriotism for the land of his birth."

"Maybe his father died fighting for his country," Gen. Spangler suggested.

"Maybe," Ms. Amann responded.

"I like it," Gen. Spangler said. "But what exactly is the Valentine's Day plot that Will Smith has to thwart?"

"They usually bring in the Wibberleys for that," Ms. Amann responded. "I do the relationship [material]."

Gen. Spangler rebriefed the group on the purpose of the session, requesting that they leave aside for the moment who might be behind such actions and focus on the mechanics of the actions themselves. "Everything follows from character," Ms. Amann responded. "You're going to end up with a Michael Bay movie."

"I'm not good at pitching," Ms. Sunset apologized, "but, anyhoo, just, well, here I go, my idea: Evil genius, Muhammad Allah Ding-Dong, Fu Manchu, whoever, is releasing these videotapes, which of course CNN, MSNBC, everybody is airing ad nauseam, right? Turns out he's *hypnotizing* everybody, so it's the first game of the World Series, we're all singing 'Star-Spangled Banner'—*and the home of the braaaave....* That's the trigger: Suddenly everybody wants to kill the president of the United States. Two hundred million people, Congress, even the Secret Service...."

"*Except*," Gen. Spangler interjected. "Except the one agent who's *too stupid* to be hypnotized."

"Steve Carell!" Mr. Duckler suggested. Ms. Amann cited a recent *Entertainment Weekly* interview in which Mr. Carell stated his desire to leave "dumb guy" roles behind. "He's an *American,* isn't he?" Mr. Duckler responded, then told Ms. Sunset to definitely call him after the meeting.

"One goddamn second," Gen. Spangler said. "I was the one who came up with the key comic conceit. Without the dumb guy there's no movie."

Mr. Duckler began to lecture Gen. Spangler on "how this business works" but was interrupted when three MPs dragged him from the room.

After a short silence, Mr. McBoog spoke for the first time. "I always wondered," he said, "What would happen if ~~rather than going for a big smash they just went for a small~~ ~~thing stronger~~ ~~softer.~~ It could be something as simple as ~~getting off the chair, going~~ ~~really really slow. There really~~ or maybe ~~some~~ ~~thing so devilishly clever that~~ ~~it's hard to do in here, even~~ ~~under all this black.~~"

The meeting was adjourned. Mr. McBoog was asked to stay behind.

How to Handle Your Money

Go to the bank and get all of your money. Accept only uncirculated singles. Come home. Lock doors and windows, unplug phones and appliances, and place electrical tape over sockets.

Draw the blinds. Put on latex gloves.

Place bills face ·down. With a Magic Marker, black out the Eye of Horus above the Masonic pyramid. Fill in the oval completely.

Secure your money, avoiding obvious spots such as under mattresses, behind paintings, up your or your spouse's anus, in cookie jars, etc. Suggested hiding places:

- Spread out in a single layer behind the wallpaper
- Colored with crayons and taped to refrigerator

- Folded and frozen into ice cubes
- Sewn inside dog

Spread your money across several different locations, keep-
ing all of them in sight at all times. Stand with your feet eighteen
inches apart, knees slightly bent, ready to spring in any direction.
Remain very still.

Thank You for Considering My Cult

You picked a great day to visit. We have meat on Sundays.

Meat! Meat! Meat! Meat! . . .

Ignore those guys. They're nuts. C'mon, let me show you around. I think you're going to love it here.

If you don't mind, could I ask how you heard about us? It wasn't *Nightline*? That Cynthia McFadden, oh boy. She draws you into those dreamy green pools of hers, and next thing you know you're saying all sorts of bizarre crap. Creepy, how she does that.

Don't step in that bejeweled area. I spat there once and some consider it "sacred ground." They'd kill you before I could stop them.

So you know, then: we are the Mighties of David, after the ragtag band of warriors the giant-slayer assembled to battle the

Elders of Zion. I'm David, but not that David. It's just a happy co-incidence.

Hey, Eleazar, Son of Dodai! One of my top Mighties, this fella, in charge of explosives and root vegetables. You can shake his hand, perfectly safe. We do all our own prosthetics here; our guy, Abishai the Extremity Maker, did the arm for the first *Terminator.* Those knuckles are fully articulated, by the way. Don't worry; it won't crush you.

Okay, broad strokes: We're a democracy up here. How we do that is we achieve a consensus through me, which I pronounce and it's written in stone, then tossed on the Pile of David. Bigger stone means bigger law. A few of the biggest: Tithing is 80 percent, *before agency commissions;* sexual activity is permitted, pending my availability on a first come first served basis; and, well, those are the two big ones.

Over in this area are the sleeping pits, and right next to that is the prayer/jerk circle—still a couple open spots if you're interested, right next to Benaiah the Grub Hunter or Jashobeam the Ant Piper, or you could squeeze in between Shammah the Sin Eater and Zalmon the Body Cleanser, sons of Anthony Quinn, the Zorba the Greek.

Well, maybe later then.

Okay, those tents, right to left: latrine, abattoir, showers, canteen. We've got to get some signs up. And down there, through those trees, you can see the lake where they shot the opening to the old *Andy Griffith Show.*

Ooh, sorry, didn't see you, Eliphelet! Of all of my Mighties, all of whom would give an arm or a leg, none have given as much or as generously as Eliphalet the Frequently Chosen.

You just sort of tug on his ear.

Our beliefs? You know, it's funny; most people don't even ask that. Pretty basic. We're fighting the Elders of Zion, who control the means of production through wickedness and vertical integration. That's why we're ideally situated up here in the hills; we can make sorties at will against Paramount to the south and Disney and Universal in the Valley; Fox and Sony are less than a day's march. Interesting note: this whole encampment was once owned by another king, King Vidor. And later by Sheila E. Frankie Muniz donated it when he joined. I'd introduce you, but he's in the Enlightenment Box right now, learning the meaning of *off the top.*

Now, I don't want you to get the impression that this is some sort of fantasy paradise. I mean, it's a great space and this is the swellest bunch of guys, and gal. But we're in an epic struggle here. This time it really is David versus Goliath. Thus, the pile of stones.

Meat . . . meat . . . meat . . .

They do love their meat. And they've earned it. Can you stay for dinner?

Wonderful. Listen, could you reach into this bladder and pull out a pebble?

It's a tradition.

No, you're our guest, you go first. Any pebble.

You got the red one! And on your first try.

Meat! . . . Meat! . . . Meat! . . . Meat! . . .

Welcome, Brother. Let's eat.

Due to numerous factors that retailers can't control, 2008 has been a challenging year and it seems this pattern will continue throughout the crucial holiday shopping season.

—Bill Martin, cofounder of ShopperTrak

Is There a Problem Here?

Yes. Yes, there is. I go to the trouble of driving all the way across town, through three restricted zones, one of them Magenta, just to do my Christmas shopping at your mall, and you expect me to pay for parking?

So then the only space I can find is next to Macy's, which is still on fire, by the way, and a mile from any of the open stores. Do you know how aggravating it is running past all those cars in primo spots, abandoned and overrun with snakes?

Radio Shack is out of everything: generators, shortwaves, water-filtration units, Tasers, Kevorkians, D batteries . . . Dude says try the Hammacher Schlemmer, and then just starts laughing. They won't even let me in the Gap. You have to be a registered Christian to wear their clothes now, apparently. Girl explains it'll make it easier for Jesus at the Rapture. And Petco only has "humane" snake traps. Screw that.

Anyway, the main reason I'm here is to acquire a little Christmas cheer for the wife, and, while I'm at it, something to maybe perk up our love life, which took a major hit when we lost the bedroom furniture to marauders. Victoria's Secret is empty, on account of The Great Sloughing, I suppose. But I still can't get any service. The girl behind the counter, vacant, practically drooling, shows no interest in my wife's particular lingerie needs. Instead, she offers to take me into a dressing room and try on some outfits for me, at which point I realize, duh, she's a zombie, and I have to take her out. The manager yells at me for not using my silencer, and then says they don't accept American Express, or anything American.

Oh, and hey, that Santa of yours? A lot of kids going into his little house, not a lot coming out. Zombie. I'm just saying.

I decide to grab a bite from your food court before I go, because, you never know, right? And that's when I started screaming and shooting things until you came over here. Look at this Southwest Wrap.

What's wrong with it is you're not supposed to taste the snake.

No, you're not. Someone forgot to put on the Special Masking Sauce.

Well, if you're out of Special Masking Sauce you should put up a sign or something. And check out these Curly Fries.

They're not curly. They're barely even twisted. Watch. When I hold one up, it goes completely limp. But you don't care.

You asked, Is there a problem here? There's your answer. That's the problem. When you stopped worrying about the curliness of your fries, when workers like you stopped worrying about the curliness, or creaminess, or deadliness of their respective fries, that's when this country got on the wrong track; that's when the bankers and CEOs all disappeared into that underground paradise they've been building since the eighties; that's when women's skin started falling off; that's when the Treasury Department, in a last-ditch effort to solve the financial crisis, certified all Monopoly and other board-game moneys; that's when the rivers ran red, and gelatinous, with what many thought was strawberry Jell-O but really, really was not; that's when the post office finally followed through on its threats to stop Saturday delivery; that's when dogs mated with cats, producing a pet that was unfriendly yet still slobbered all over you; that's when the president and the Congress went on a fact-finding mission to Subterrania and never came back; that's when baboons gained speech but only used it to make hurtful comments; that's when the dead rose and flooded the job market with cheap, disposable labor, and the serpents, seeing an opening, took dominion over this once great nation of ours.

You and your uncurled fries.

Oh, yeah, sure. *And* the asteroid. Let's all blame the asteroid.

Pieces
Left Out
of This
Collection

Selecting pieces for a humor collection is a bit like choosing which of your children will live or die, less histrionic perhaps, but still tricky. Do you exclude a piece simply because it is poorly written, or not funny? Evidently not. But to include everything would require several volumes, printed on fine Bible paper handsewn into black calfskin with bound-in silk bookmarks, no skimping on the gilt. And that won't be happening with my current publisher.

On the following pages is a small sampling of the hard work that I decided, drinking heavily, to leave out of this collection. You may disagree. If so, I encourage you to call Rupert Murdoch and insist these pieces be included in the next edition. And mention the calfskin.

*Some jokes don't age well. Like ones premised on the World Trade Center bomb-
ing (the first, hilarious, one). Or which attack a disgraced public official who
has since become beloved, on account of being dead. Or which make a reduc-
tio ad absurdum argument about American capitalism, never a good bet. In-
cluding such a ludicrously outdated piece in this collection would have only
served to remind readers that the author is old, making them sad.*

A Government informer and the man charged with
leading a foiled plot to bomb New York City targets
discussed abducting former president Richard M.
Nixon . . . in a hostage-taking scheme aimed at winning
release of Muslims being held in Federal custody in
connection with the bombing of the World Trade
Center last February [1993].

    Mr. Nixon, who lives in New Jersey, could not be
reached for comment.

—New York Times

You Won't Have Nixon to Kick Around Anymore, Dirtbag

LOS ANGELES, Sept. 20—"The Taking of the President: The Terrorist Abduction of Richard M. Nixon," a political thriller to be written by Mr. Nixon, will be on sale December 6, Simon and Schuster announced today.

The book, as yet unfinished, will be published in trade paperback as part of the Richard Nixon Library series, under the publisher's Touchstone Books imprint, according to Touchstone spokeswoman Lynda Coover.

"Taking," based on an alleged real-life terrorist plot to kidnap Mr. Nixon and exchange him for Muslims being held in connection with the World Trade Center bombing, will chronicle the hypothetical abduction and the former president's presumed subsequent daring escape, said Ms. Coover, who spells her given name with a "y" for professional reasons.

Mr. Nixon has written eight other books since leaving office in 1974, but Ms. Coover emphasized that this was the first time the former president has dabbled in fiction.

"Though I hesitate to call it fiction," she added. "As I understand it, they [the alleged terrorists] had discussed this, perhaps even planned it—I don't know. But what Mr. Nixon has done, is doing as we speak, is reconstructing the actual events as they might have actually transpired. Call it 'speculative nonfiction.'"

Simon and Schuster was criticized this summer for publishing Joe McGinniss's "The Last Brother," a biography of Senator Edward Kennedy that included thoughts and emotions the senator had not had, but Ms. Coover maintained that Mr. Nixon's book would be different. "It will contain only Mr. Nixon's authentic thoughts and feelings, captured as he is thinking or feeling them while writing the book," she said. A movie based on the book is also in the works, said Kym Brooder, a spokeswoman for Paramount Communications Inc., Simon and Schuster's parent company. "We find the idea of a former American president as action hero to be very, very exciting," said Ms. Brooder, who changed the "i" to a "y" as a teenager and it simply stuck.

"Executive in Action: Expletive Deleted," based on Mr. Nixon's screenplay and scheduled for release in early summer 1994, will be directed by Sidney Pollack, who helmed Paramount Pictures' 1993 summer blockbuster "The Firm." Mr. Pollack was criticized for taking liberties with John Grisham's bestselling book, but Ms. Brooder did not see that issue arising in this case "because Dick's not a control freak."

In the film, which will emphasize action elements of the book over its geopolitical insights, the part of Mr. Nixon will be played by Dan Aykroyd, star of "Coneheads," another Paramount release. Mr. Aykroyd, whose affectionate portrayal of Mr. Nixon on NBC's "Saturday Night Live" made an indelible impression on the former president, stepped into the role when Mr. Nixon's first choice, George C. Scott, was unavailable. Instead of relying on time-consuming and cumbersome makeup to transform Mr. Aykroyd into Mr. Nixon, "morphing" technology will be used to superimpose Mr. Nixon's face directly onto Mr. Aykroyd's. "The face will be Dick's but the acting will be all Dan's," Ms. Brooder said.

Next fall will also see Mr. Nixon's book turned into a four-part, six-hour syndicated miniseries, according to Paramount Television spokeswoman Lyssa Dooley, who swears that's how it's spelled on her birth certificate. Ms. Dooley promised that the television version would differ significantly from both the book and movie version in that "it's set five hundred years in the future, for starters.

"Also, the story will involve several characters and settings from 'The Next Generation' universe," she said, referring to Paramount's immensely popular syndicated series, "Star Trek: The Next Generation." Mr. Nixon, reportedly "a big Trekker," will pen the teleplay, and is "noodling with" the notion of doing "a holographic cameo," Ms. Dooley said. Plot details have yet to be worked out, she said, but added that the Muslim terrorists would likely be replaced by "some sort of alien entity."

"niXon: the X-President #1," a 32-page full-color comic book to be written and drawn by Mr. Nixon, will debut in November 1994, according to Paramount licensing spokesman Byll Germane, who admits it's "a bit of an affectation." "niXon" will mix elements from the book, movie, and series, in addition to which Mr. Nixon will have as yet undetermined superpowers. Images from the comic book will also be reproduced on a set of Day-Glo posters and in a series of Bahamian commemorative stamps.

The Christmas 1994 shopping season will feature covert-action figures based on the comic, Mr. Germane said, as well as a multiplayer interactive online game based on the miniseries, and, based on the book itself, toys for the tub.

Had I included the following piece in this collection, careful readers might have complained about similarities between it and "Freezer Madness" (p. 211). They might even have speculated that after failing to sell a tasteless Roald Dahl rip-off that makes light of a notorious double murder, I changed the title and lead quote, recast it as a drug-education spoof, and foisted it on unsuspecting editors at Esquire. *But this kind of debate is more properly dealt with in a dissertation, or monograph, or hagiography, and has no place in a perhaps award-winning humor collection.*

JOHNNIE COCHRAN: Officer, would you agree with me that the best evidence of the condition of that ice cream, when you first saw it on that night, would be a picture of how it looked? Isn't that correct?

OFFICER RISKE: A picture of when I actually saw it, yes.

COCHRAN: When you saw it, yes. We don't have that, do we?

RISKE: Not that I know of.

COCHRAN: What kind of container of ice cream was this?

RISKE: It was like a cardboard Ben & Jerry's container.

COCHRAN: Ben & Jerry's?

RISKE: Ben & Jerry's.

—*The People v. O. J. Simpson*

CHUBBY HUBBY—Chocolate Covered Peanut Butter Filled Pretzels in Vanilla Malt Ice Cream Rippled with Fudge & Peanut Butter

—New Ben & Jerry's flavor

Farewell, My Chubby

He was in there, getting fatter. From the kitchen she could see only a couple pounds of him, his big fat head bulging out atop the chair, his little fat fingers hanging like sausages off the armrest. Beyond that, there was only the television, and football, again.

It had been like this ever since ScrImage Online. *The football you want. When you want it.* And he wanted it all the time. Their Internet bills were ridiculous. Today it was the '73 Bills against the '63 Bears in old Soldier Field, for the third time this week. O. J. Simpson had just broken a Mike Ditka tackle, and Ditka was standing there, his helmet lolling strangely back, the front of his jersey turning a glistening ruby red.

—Jesus Christ, is anybody gonna *call* that? her husband yelled at the screen, the top of his head bobbing up and down excitedly like, it occurred to her, a monkey's butt. She giggled. It would only be a matter of time now. He would scream. For ice cream.

Chapter Two

As she swung the huge stainless-steel cart around the corner and to the long gleaming freezer case, she realized she hated him. He hated all the flavors. He would eat them, of course, but he would complain the whole time. So she had spent two hours in her grocer's freezer section searching for a flavor he had never had. He had had a lot of flavors.

Forget the Classics: vanilla, strawberry, chocolate. Those aren't flavors, he said, they're *ingredients*. She moved on, quickly past Literary—Huckleberry Sinn, Glacé Menagerie—"egghead cream," he called them. And also past Bestsellers—the Bridge Mix of Madison County, the Celestine Recipe—he mocked her for eating those, but she knew: they made him feel stupid as well. As she passed Mystery, she looked away, hating him. They had once curled up together with a pint of Double Chocolate Indemnity and two spoons, but now the sound of her spoon clicking his gave him an ice cream headache, he said.

Over in the next aisle, more his speed, was Movies and TV—Mama Gump Chunk, Yum 'n Yummer, NYPB Blue—but nothing he hadn't had a hundred times in the past month. The same in Celebrity—Madonna Cioccalato—and Current Events—White Chocolate Bronco, Uncle Newt's Old Fashioned Vanilla 'n Cream. *Ate it, hate it, ate it, hate it, ate it,* she pre-scolded herself, clawing through the pints, her fingers burning with cold. Leaning over, she dug deeper, to the frost-crusted containers in the back. She scraped the ice away with her thumbnail: Kerrigan Krunch. *Doesn't anyone check the expiration dates on these things?* she thought, tossing a Bobbitt Split back into the freezer case. A stack of Chewy Buttafuoco toppled over, and then, there, in white type on a black label:

CHUBBY HUBBY

There was one left. She grabbed it and read the label. *Chocolate Covered Peanut Butter Filled Pretzels.* It made her feel ill. He would love it. It was only then that she noticed how heavy it was. And hard.

Chapter Three

—*Ice cream!* he screamed.

—*Ice cream,* she chirped back, hopping off her stool. She giggled again as she opened the refrigerator door. It had been in there all afternoon, in the very back of the freezer against the coils, getting harder. He would have such an ice cream headache. Later, when the police arrived, it would be soft enough for spooning. Perhaps the nice officers would like some. Like in that horrid flavor, what was it called? *Roald Dahl's Murder by Sweet.* She couldn't stop giggling.

She reached in, pushing aside the long-abandoned Lean Cuisines, deep into the freezer. Stifling a cackle, she pulled out the container. It was empty. The spoon was still inside. She *Hello, we're Ben and Jerry, and we really must protest at this point. We know what the author is trying to do, and we don't like it one bit. To our knowl-edge, a Ben & Jerry's prepacked pint has never been used in the com-mission of a first-degree murder. And let us reiterate that the link between premium ice cream and violence is tenuous at best. Millions of Americans enjoy our fresh, delicious ice cream regularly and the vast majority of them do not kill their spouses.*

It's not always easy to tell when you're creating child pornography. Back when I was at the National Lampoon, I got this idea for an illustrated satire of achievement parenting and the DIY movement. The lawyer informed me if the piece ran, however, what few advertisers we had left would storm the office and stomp us dead. He cited a wacky child pornography spoof they had run years earlier, involving adult midgets pretending to be toddlers and engaged in various sex acts. I felt my piece wasn't that bad. Yet even though it never ran, and I was fired shortly thereafter, the magazine was still stomped dead less than six months later. So, obviously, I couldn't take the chance of including it in this collection.

Protecting Your Baby Investment*

Congratulations! You're a new father! Let's have a look at your investment so far:

$27,585.75

---

* *Cf.* "The Babyproofer" (p. 166), which was written *after* I had a child.

Of course this does not include start-up (e.g., courting costs, rings, wedding expenses due to father-in-law default, honeymoon, etc.), which must be amortized across future babies, nor does it take into account baby-driven increases in your overhead (e.g., moving to a baby-friendly neighborhood, upgrading the help). Nevertheless, even as a lowball estimate, this figure should make one point exceedingly clear: you've put a whole lot of money into this baby. And right about now you may be asking yourself, "Was a baby the smartest investment we could have made in these uncertain times?"

The answer, unequivocally, is yes. A baby is *always* a smart investment, because a baby *continues to grow regardless of the economic climate*!

But there's one important caveat: to capitalize your baby, you must carry it for a term of eighteen to twenty-one years, and sometimes more, until it reaches full maturity. Expect some rough sledding along the way; babies are extraordinarily vulnerable ventures, particularly in the first six to eighteen quarters when they are subject to any number of risks, including but not limited to electrical outlets, stairs, and open fire pits. Protecting your baby investment therefore requires diligence, ingenuity, and more than a little old-fashioned elbow grease.

YOUR BABY'S HEAD: THE HEART OF THE OPERATION

While there are certainly some exceptions, your baby's head—and specifically its brain—is a crucial factor in determining long-term future dividends. Unfortunately, your baby's "profit center" is ill-protected by its natural casing, which, due to a manufacturing defect, is soft and mushy. One way to compensate for this structural flaw is to buy commercial infant headgear (available at most baby sporting goods stores) and have your baby wear it at all times. Bear in mind, however, that in July 1991, a woman in Ojai, California, stopped her bicycle suddenly to avoid hitting a squirrel, turned around, and was horrified to discover her twenty-two-month-old son with his Babyguard® ToddlerTopper™ *dangerously askew.* While it's true that this product was quickly recalled and that the company was subsequently litigated out of existence, it's also true that *no* infant headgear on the market today has been designed using your baby's precise cranial specifications.

However, you can do this *yourself,* at home, and for less than five dollars. First, purchase a 16" square of 2"-thick foam padding (depending on the size of your baby's head and his propensity for banging it into things, you may want to go with 3" foam) and "mold" it to your baby's head [Fig. A]. Secure the foam in place by wrapping it completely with any commercial packing tape [Fig. B], then trim the excess foam. Tuck the whole thing into an attractive bonnet [Fig. C] and it's hardly noticeable. It also can be disassembled at any time, before bathing for instance, although this is neither necessary nor advisable.

INTO THE MOUTHS AND EYES OF BABES

Babies are naturally curious. An admirable trait perhaps, but the downside is that a baby's curiosity is directed almost exclusively at objects that choke, poison, pinch, cut, bruise, burn, irritate, infect, abrade, blind, or are expensive to replace, thus setting into motion the toxic cycle of blame and guilt that will lead inexorably to your baby dysfunctioning down the road and deciding to become an artist—in other words, an emotional loss leader and chronic income siphon. An entire industry has sprung up preying on these fears, marketing devices that allegedly "babyproof" your home— outlet plugs, cabinet latches, cable lock boxes—but these contraptions can be easily circumvented by clever babies, and certainly by any baby worth having.

Again, you can do better than store-bought, and for far less money. You will need four ¼" x ⅝" metal plates, about 12" of coated copper wire, a 12-volt battery, a roll of electrical tape, and a small electronic buzzer, horn, or siren. Fully insulate the baby's hands and then tape two plates onto each palm about ¹⁄₁₆" apart [Fig. D] Run wires up along the arms to the power source/soundmaker assembly, located on the baby's back [Fig. E]. Each time your baby picks up a dangerous metal object, the completed circuit will set off the soundmaker, alerting you and nonverbally communicating to the baby that the object should be dropped [Fig. F]. You can extend this deterrent effect throughout your household by wrapping stripped copper wire around bottles of cleansers, drugs, and other items you do not wish your baby to touch (your Blu-ray, for example). Which noises are most effective vary from baby to baby; you will want to experiment. Also, top-notch babies will quickly acclimate to particular sounds, and may even begin to enjoy making them, so be prepared to vary the sound and volume frequently. But try to stay away from low, harsh buzzers or horns, which can sound overly judgmental.

DEFENDING YOUR BABY'S PRIVATE ENTERPRISE

While maintaining your baby's reproductive organs has no direct bearing on your investment return (on the contrary, reproduction-driven babies sometimes choose to reinvest profits in babies of their own rather than paying much-deserved dividends), it is nevertheless critical to preserve the integrity of this area. Unauthorized tampering with your baby's reproductive organs can result in a devalued baby content to spend its life in some go-nowhere civil service job; or, worse, continued abuse can produce a downtown performance artist—in other words, an economic sinkhole.

Protecting your baby's private enterprise from unwanted public intervention can be accomplished inexpensively using items purchasable through several mail-order hunting catalogs.

As seen in Figure G, a spring-loaded animal trap (0–6 months, rabbit; 7–12 months, fox; 12 months and up, bear) is doubled back on itself and concealed by decoy diaper flaps. With most models, the spring mechanism can be adjusted to wound, cripple, or amputate unauthorized personnel who transgress the area.

OTHER DANGERS

But what, you may ask, about prowlers; kidnappers; drunk drivers; hurricanes; serial killers; biker gangs; falling plaster; gypsies; botulism; freaked-out junkies; wounded fugitives; Satan worshippers; bricks hurled through windows; disturbed, maternally fixated young women; teen punks out for sick fun; giant sinkholes that houses are sometimes inadvertently built over; old lovers driven insane by your happiness; boulders; anti-family terrorists; small plastic parts; twisted nannies; ball lightening; psychotic nurses; rampaging postal workers; rifts in the space-time continuum; cannibals; in the northern United States, wolves; in the Southwest, rattlesnakes; in the Everglades, gators; on the Lower East Side, ferrets; and in more American homes than ever before, cats—any or all of which might strike while you're in the bathroom with the hair dryer going? Good question.

The answer, sadly, is this: Babies are a risk. That's the nature of the business. Given the long-term rewards they offer, most investment counselors agree that they are an acceptable risk; nevertheless, you should be prepared for the possibility that one day you may glance away, only for a moment, and when you look back, your baby will be gone and all the time and money and emotion you've invested will have gone, for what? You may want to limit your exposure accordingly.

Also, just to be on the safe side, buy a gun and teach your baby how to use it.

Reading your old stuff yields the occasional small pleasure—a bit of ferocious naïveté or idiosyncratic phrasing that was possible before you became a bitter hack. But also gastrointestinal distress, as provoked by the piece below. While it certainly illustrates the dangers of writing while crying, including it in the collection would have led to further demands that I finally get help, and so I had to leave it out.

Material[*]

Thank you. Thank you. Oh, I don't deserve your love. You're too good for me. What I really need is a bigger, better-looking audience that can satisfy me sexually.

---

[*] *Cf.* "I Killed Them in New Haven" (p. 71), a later version without the excruciation.

Good night! Drive safe!

Thank you. That was just a little scene from something I'm working on. I call it, "My Love Life."

Hey.

You know, I'm really excited to be here at Laffies tonight, talking to all you folks, because I just broke up with my girlfriend—she got the dog and I got the material. I hope you enjoy it as much as I did. I tried some of it out on my good friend Lucy about four o' clock the other morning, and she says to me, "You know, Larry, maybe you should be talking to a therapist about this," and I say, "But he always laughs in the wrong places," and she says, "Okay, then that'll be eighty-five dollars."

Heyyy. Maybe I should have taken the dog.

You probably know my girlfriend. You can't miss her. She's right there at the center of the fucking universe. No, I don't mean that. Actually, she's very sweet. Here, let me tell you a little bit about my girlfriend—

Ex-girlfriend? What are you, the prefix police? No, no, I mean, thank you, sir. You are right, of course. Ex-girlfriend. Ex-girlfriend. Ex-girlfriend. Ex-girlfriend. I think I've got that now. And who is that with you tonight, sir? Your girlfriend? Well, let's be technically correct here. She's your future ex-girlfriend, right? So what's your future ex-girlfriend's name, sir? Huh? Don't you know? You, sweetheart, whatever your name is, hate to tell you this, but that's a bad sign.

My former future ex-girlfriend's name is Barb. As in Barbarian. Barbed wire. Barbecued heart on a stick. No, no, actually it's short for Barbara, of course. That's a beautiful name, don't you think? Bar-ba-ra. I call her my little yellow flower. She's so beautiful she . . .

So my girlfriend, ex-girlfriend, is a teacher. Are there any teachers out there? You, ma'am? *Fuck you!* No, no, I love teachers. But I have a question for you. You've got kids around you all day long—why would you want one of your own at home? I mean, isn't twenty-six enough? Don't you see the kind of pressure you're putting . . .

Where was I? Oh, yes, Barbara. She's so cute; she's always really concerned about her weight. Now, I'm not saying she's fat or anything, but she does have her own gravitational field. It's slight, but with the sensitive instruments they have available today—if you throw a dozen doughnuts at her at just the right angle they make rings, like Saturn.

Oh God. I can't believe—I shouldn't have said that. It's not fair. She really works so hard on it. And it's really not true. She has a beautiful face. Really. Her eyes . . .

Anyway, we broke up after three years. Guys, have you ever noticed that when a woman wants to break up with you, she has this secret female code she uses? Like, she starts saying things like, "You'll never change." Change into what? Superman? Or how about this one: "I can't take much more of this." This? *This.* Could you possibly be less specific?

Or, and guys, how many times have you heard this one: "I don't love you anymore." Yeah, right. I'm, like, "No, what is it, really?" And so finally you drag it out of her, and she says, "I want to see other people." And I'm, like, "Great! You want to see other people? I can be other people!"

Who do you want to see? A celebrity, like Regis Philbin? *Hey, I'm so much in love with you it's driving me crazy! I'm outta control!*

Thank you.

I say, Hey, you want to see some big strong hunky guy like Arnold Schwarzenegger? I can do that. *You'll be back. Hasta mañana, baby.* Or how about, I know how much you like that movie *The Quiet Man*, it always makes you cry, is that how you want me to act? *There'll be no locks and bolts between us, Barbara Kate, except those in your own mercenary heart.* Is that what you want? Me to just take you by the arm and throw you . . .

I'm sorry. Give me a second here.

Hey. Let's change gears, shall we? So I go into this convenience store to buy a pack of cigarettes—I don't smoke them anymore; I just watch them burn—and this guy behind the counter, he doesn't speak any English at all. I mean not a word, not even, for example, "cigarette." So I talked to him for about six hours about Barb. He didn't seem to mind. Really nice guy.

Funny story.

I ran into Barb on the way over here, strangely enough right in front of her house.

And I say, "Hey, I know you . . ."

And she says, "Larry, one hundred yards. The restraining order specifically—"

"Wait, wait," I say. "Aren't you . . . ? Aren't you the one? Yes, you are, aren't you, the one who recently caused a cosmic rift in the universe that will soon bring life as we know it to a cold dark end?"

"They've added extra patrols," she says. "I haven't seen one drive by in a while, so it's only a matter of time . . ."

"It has been a long time, hasn't it, Barb?"

And she says, "I gave 'em your U of I sweatshirt—for the canine unit."

"How long has it been, Barb? Since you broke my heart into more than one hundred noninterlocking pieces? How long do you think?"

"Nine days."

"So you're counting 'em, too, huh? Wow. Nine days. That's almost two weeks. Two whole weeks . . . My, my . . . Isn't that something?

"You know," I say. "I never found anybody else."

"Maybe you should try another block," Barb says.

"So, Barb," I say. "It's not too late to come crawling back, you know."

"No, thank you," she says.

So I say, "I don't want to have to beg, Barb."

"Good," she says.

"I have more dignity than that," I say. "I shouldn't have to beg for anything. *Please, please, PLEASE, don't make me beg!*"

So now I'm down on my knees, because, you know, it feels right, and I really feel like I'm making my case: "You hate me! You hate me! You hate me! You hate me! You hate me! You hate me! You hate me! You hate me! You hate me! You hate me! You hate me! You hate me! You hate me! You hate me! You hate me!"

She looks down and she says, "Larry, I don't hate you."

"You still love me! You love me! You love me! You love me! You love me!"

She looks down at me and she says softly, "Larry, this is humiliating."

She's cracking, I can see that. I've got her now, right? I break out my big guns.

"I'm worthless! I'm a worm! I'm a worthless worm! I don't know why you ever liked me! I'm so worthless and wormy! Why? Why'd you ever go out with me in the first place?"

She looks down at me with those big brown eyes and she says:

"You make me laugh."

And I just look up at her, tears in my eyes, for effect, and I say: *"But I can't be this funny all the time!"*

Thank you. Thank you. Thank you all so very much.

Thanks a lot. I think this really helped. The rest of the week you can catch me on the corner of Jane and Greenwich, muttering to myself, and then this Saturday I'll be at Nuts and Dolts in Nutley, New Jersey. Before I go, I'd like to leave you with one thought: If you can't be with the one you love, get a better lawyer than the one I got.

Good night! Drive safe!

This is my favorite humor piece. The only problem with it is that it isn't funny. (Also, "Bad Dog" [p. 174] is the inverse, or converse, or obverse of it). And so it is with great regret that I must exclude it from this collection.

How to Talk to Your Dog[*]

Have you ever noticed that you always know when your dog wants to go "out"? Or when he is hungry? Or when he is angry with you or others?

You know because your dog is *already* talking to you!

Dogs are natural actors, instinctively adept at using their bodies and facial expressions to communicate with you *nonverbally*. They are also expert mimes, capable of performing a vast

---

[*] Like He's Your Best Friend

repertoire of deceptively simple routines to subtly get their points across. Some of these "bits" are universal (e.g., nosing the dog dish to indicate hunger, drinking out of the toilet to indicate thirst), but most are specific to the dog. For example, my own dog, Flynn (a seven-year-old Irish setter), raises his paw and points at the television screen when he wants me to change the channel.

Many dog owners are content to communicate with their pets solely on this preverbal level. But imagine how handy it would be if, in addition to being able to alert you when somebody was at the door, your dog could also tell you who it was (dogs, remember, have a keen sense of smell). Or how enriching your relationship with your dog would be if the two of you could just "shoot the breeze" sometimes.

You will learn more about how to do this in the next chapter.

EXERCISES: Try this simple nonverbal exchange: place both hands firmly on either side of your dog's head. Apply firm pressure and pull your dog's face close to yours (between 1" and 2" is optimum). Now, smile broadly and—again, using both hands—vigorously stroke your dog in an upward motion from the base of his neck to just behind his ears. Your dog will understand this as meaning, "I like you. I value you as my dog." If your dog then licks your face, that means, "I like you, too!" (Do not be discouraged if your dog does not immediately lick your face. The setting may be too intimate for him, or, more likely, he is just not a licker.)

THE CANINE TONGUE

Dogs are the most vocal of all domesticated animals. Whereas the cat goes meow, the cow goes moo, the sheep goes baa, and the pig goes oink-oink, the dog is not limited by these crude utterances.

The average American dog can bark, howl, yap, snap, growl, whimper, woof, yelp, bay, howl, whine, gnarl, mutter, and, of course, bow-wow. In fact, many scientists believe that if dogs had more highly developed brains and sophisticated vocal cords, they could converse much like humans do.

But make no mistake: dogs do "speak," and not just as a parlor trick. My own close examination of the canine tongue reveals that dogs have a "vocabulary" in excess of 2,000 words. Fortunately, nearly all of these words roughly translate into the English word "food" (dogs have more than 120 words for dry food alone), and so you will only need to learn a working vocabulary of about 400 words in order to talk to your dog.

Pronunciation can be tricky, however. The canine alphabet differs significantly from ours, featuring a fraction of our consonants (*b, f, h, p, r, w,* and sometimes *y*) and the rounder vowel sounds, which are more "sung" than "spoken." Words are therefore primarily distinguished by minor variations in pronunciation (dogs can differentiate twelve types of *r* sounds and five degrees of hardness in the letter *b*). From this deceptively sparse phoneme palette, dogs are thus able to create a comparatively rich language.

A basic Canine/English dictionary can be found at the back of this book, but you should be aware of few matters of form and style before attempting to use it.

Eschew Excess Barking. Dogs tend to follow *Strunk and White*'s dictum about omitting needless words and avoiding weak modifiers. Rather than saying something smells "very tasty," a dog will simply bark "tasty" (*woh-af*), placing added emphasis on the initial vowel sound and saying the entire word louder.

Regarding Plurals and Possessives. There is no true plural in the canine tongue. Rather, your dog, seeing another dog, may say, *Rarf!* ("Hey, there's another dog!"), whereas, upon seeing a pack of dogs, your dog will likely exclaim: *Rarf rarf rarf rarf rarf rarf!* Possessives, on the other hand, are usually indicated with a low growl.

Some Things Just Won't Translate. Not all human concepts are meaningful to dogs; for instance, there is no dog word for "stay." Likewise, there are several dog phrases which cannot be translated adequately into English (a few of these do have analogues in German and Chinese, however). Among the more enigmatic dogisms you are likely to encounter:

Bow wow—This frequently uttered canine cant provides an intriguing look at your dog's overall philosophy. Directly translated into English, *bow wow* means, simply, "I am." But to your dog, it means something ineffably more.

Rowp! Rowp!—Usually delivered enthusiastically with your dog's head thrown back, means something along the order of "Would you listen to that? Is that loud or what?"

Rur rar roo roo roo rawr rawr awr raw rarp rarp rarp!—Means nothing; your dog has gone crazy.

EXERCISES: Let's start with a simple "hello." While dogs prefer to say hello nonverbally, they are capable of a standard declarative greeting when actual contact is not possible. The dog word for "hello" is *woof* (pronounced *wuf, wüf,* and sometimes *wrüf,* depending on breed and regional dialect). Facing your dog, say *woof* in as energetically and friendly a way as possible (tone of voice is very important; the similar-sounding *weuf* means "Back off! This is my food!"). For maximum impact, place added emphasis on the *w* and *f* sounds (The *f* is actually more of a *ph*. Dogs have more space between their lips and teeth than humans do, which causes increased "lip flapping" when they speak and makes them particularly well-suited for consonantal diphthongs.) If you have said "hello" correctly, your dog will *woof* back, a bit louder and slightly higher in pitch. If your dog just stares at you, you have probably mispronounced the word. Try again. If repeated attempts to say hello fail, it may be because your dog feels you are making fun or trying to talk down to him. Try to sound more sincere. If you have a smaller dog, you also might want to try substituting the phrase *yip yip yip*.

NOW THAT YOU AND YOUR DOG ARE ON SPEAKING TERMS: WHAT DO YOU TALK ABOUT?

Like humans, dogs prefer to talk about what they know. This varies widely from dog to dog, but my experience with Flynn is probably typical.

Flynn loves to talk about smells, all kinds of smells, even and especially smells humans consider impolite to discuss. You must try to give your dog some latitude in this regard. Remember, smells are your dog's only colors.

Flynn is also keenly interested in the environment, though his commitment wavers. During our trips to the city, for example, he will complain long and bitterly about the air quality, and yet, he plainly enjoys all the garbage.

Among Flynn's other favorite topics of conversation are: animals (all kinds), music (particularly opera), the weather, and the moon. Conversation stoppers for Flynn include: politics, religion, sports, clothing, the future, and money matters (about which he often displays an exasperating disinterest).

Your dog will likely share some of Flynn's interests; undoubtedly he will have several of his own. The important thing for you is to explore a full range of talking points with your dog, to discover what *he* wants to talk about. Any topic is fair game, although I would strongly warn you against broaching the subject of death. When I tried to explain this concept to Flynn, he began whimpering uncontrollably, then took off through the house, scooting along on his rear end and making a horrible mess.

EXERCISES: Take your dog for a short, brisk walk around the block. When you arrive home, go into separate rooms and compose a list of all of the things you saw. (Since your dog cannot write, he will have to memorize his.) After about fifteen minutes (a time limit is important; your dog will otherwise spend hours pondering a single five-minute walk), get together and compare and contrast your lists.

You will be amazed at how differently you and your dog look at the world.

GETTING PAST THE SMALL TALK

How much do you really know about your dog? To find out, it is not enough to talk to your dog: you must also *listen*. Only then will your true dog emerge, as Flynn has for me.

For example, I never realized, *until I took the time to listen,* that Flynn has such a terrific sense of humor (albeit a bit immature). Before I mastered his language, one of Flynn's favorite jokes was to spout a canine vulgarity of the lowest order whenever I commanded him to "speak." He's really quite a kidder.

In getting Flynn to open up, I also discovered he has the heart of a poet (as I suspect most dogs do). He loves to recite his song poems (which resemble blues dirges) on clear evenings when there is a full moon. Here's one (translated):

> My master is good
>> and he gives me good food.
> When I am hungry,
>> he brings me food then.
> Except sometimes,
>> I remember one time in particular.
> But mostly,
>> he is a good provider.

Had I known this was what Flynn had been howling all along, I never would have yelled at him to shut up. Getting to know your dog can help you avoid similar misunderstandings.

Be warned, however: it is possible you and your dog will get to know each other, only to realize you are totally incompatible. This happens rarely, but when it does, it is better to accept this fact, and take appropriate measures, than to go on living a lie.

EXERCISES: If you and your dog have gotten this far, you are beyond structured exercises.

HOW TO TALK TO A BAD DOG

Being able to talk to your dog is wonderful, but should not be confused with true intimacy. Don't find this out the hard way, as I had to.

A few months ago, I came home from work and discovered Flynn had chewed up all the mail. He could not, or would not, give any explanation for his behavior. Furthermore, he did not seem the least bit contrite. I sternly lectured him on the importance of respecting the property of others (throwing in a few ominous references to U.S. Postal Inspectors) and thought that would be the end of the matter.

But the next day, Flynn had done it again. He had also attempted to hide the results of his crime throughout the house.

It didn't take too long to figure out what was going on. Behind the bedroom toilet (where Flynn is not even supposed to go), I found the pulpy remains of my broadband bill; it was for nearly fifteen hundred dollars!

A quick call to the company confirmed my worst suspicions: *someone* had ordered *Beverly Hills Chihuahua* more than three hundred times. (This is not quite the fantastic accomplishment it seems; the remote is quite intuitive.) Although a cable company supervisor said she would give me a one-time credit on the bill, I was absolutely furious. It wasn't the money; it was that Flynn had deliberately *lied* to me, something I thought dogs were not even capable of.

I lost control and lashed out at Flynn viciously.

Harph! Harhh rrah gruh rau-hurr! I barked without thinking, and then went on to say a number of other things I immediately wished I could take back. But it was too late; Flynn had understood every word.

In retrospect, I guess I should have just taken a rolled-up newspaper and rapped Flynn across the snout. I thought we had gotten beyond that kind of thing, but I've since come to realize that words hurt far more when they are spoken in anger than when they appear on the printed page.

WHEN YOUR DOG IS NO LONGER TALKING TO YOU

Flynn didn't speak to me for a long time after the *Chihuahua* incident. I would try to initiate conversations, ask Flynn how his day was, but he would just mutter something unintelligible. When I would try to tell him how my day had gone, he would look straight into my eyes, and then rudely turn away to attend to an itch between his legs.

After about three weeks of this, I couldn't take it anymore. I got down on my knees and literally begged Flynn to talk to me again. I have re-created the resulting conversation below. It represented an important breakthrough for Flynn and me, and I think you'll find it instructive.

Me: C'mon, boy, speak to me! Speak!

Flynn: *Arph?*

Me: *Arph?* Because we need to talk about this. I'm going nuts with this.

Flynn: *Wuf wif.*

Me: I said I was sorry! You don't know how sorry I am. *Rü!* But there's something else going on here, isn't there? You can tell me, boy. This is your best friend talking. Please. *Roof.*

(long pause)

Flynn (softly): *Har hraugh rhuf whuf hrr.*

Me: What do you mean? I pay attention to you all the time!

Flynn: *Har hraugh* rhuf *whuf hrr.*

Me: Yeah, *rhuf.* We talk all the time, don't we? Or at least we used to.

Flynn: *Rhuf*... rhuf... *hurr*.

Me: Oh my God. I am such an idiot.

What I had only then realized was that when Flynn said to me, "You never pay attention to me anymore," he was *employing a euphemism!* What he had meant was, "You never *pet* me anymore." And I had completely missed it.

I had gotten so wrapped up in the idea of being able to talk to Flynn, and so comfortable discussing matters with him as an equal, I had completely forgotten that, when you get right down to it, Flynn was just a dog—a dog with the same physical and emotional needs as any dog. Words count for very little to a dog; actions speak much louder.

This is the most important lesson I can impart to you: it is not enough to talk to your dog; you must also *communicate.* I shudder to think that if Flynn had not opened up to me, I might have gone on hurting him indefinitely. Remember: *your* dog might not be as assertive.

Flynn and I talk less than we did at the beginning, but that's all right. We know that when we want to, or need to, we can. And it still comes in quite handy sometimes.

But other times, like on hot, firefly nights, when the stars seem so close you can catch them in your mouth, and the old porch swing creaks rhythmically back and forth with the crickets adding chirpy syncopation, and the slow, thick air smells a deep, dark purple, well, words are meaningless. Flynn has taught me that.

You can purchase the audiobook for your dog by sending $19.95 cash or money order plus $3.50 for postage and handling to: Talking Dog, P.O. 8745, Champaign, IL 61820. Flynn cautions that some of the growling on this tape may be too intense for younger dogs or more sensitive, miniature dogs.

Acknowledgments

There are more than fifty pieces in this book, originally published over a twenty-year period, requiring the support and services of dozens of kind and talented people. Acknowledging everyone by name, even just the ones I'm still friends with, would be prohibitively time-and-space consuming, and so I ask their indulgence as I identify them by first initial:

A(3), B(2), C(3), D(9), G(2), I, J(6), K, M(2), P, R(4), S(3), T(2), and W.

Thank you all, especially one of the J's.

Addendum to the Acknowledgments

It has been brought to my attention that my previous acknowledgments might come off as seeming unprofessional, or "dickish." *Jesus.* This is why I left them off the last book. Of course that didn't stop my friend Randy Klimpert from complaining that I quoted lyrics he may or may not have written without permission. I mean, I quoted a lot of lyrics without permission, and I don't hear Eric Clapton or David Bowie complaining.

Anyway.

This book would not have been possible if not for the tireless, brilliant, etc., efforts of my various editors, who were a joy to work with for the most part, and whose perceptive edits I have systematically reversed at my peril: Julia Just, Roger Angell, George Barkin, Diane Giddis, Sam Johnson, Chris Marcil, Ian Maxtone-Graham, David Kuhn, David Granger, Peter Griffin, Derek Haas, Cheston Knapp, and especially Susan Morrison, who edited the plurality of these pieces as she will many, many future ones, I hope. Abigail Holstein shepherded the collection itself, twisting and tweaking it into an actual book, and without her efforts there would be a lot more of a lot less. And Sarah Burnes, my brilliant agent, managed to sell the whole mess for an amount that will exceed its return by a goodly margin.

A career this long, even one this modest, requires its fair share of promoters, cheerleaders, and muses, and I number among them: Judy McGuinn, Jane Flynn-Royko, Randy Cohen, Sandy Frazier, Joanne Gruber, Cara Stein, Ron Hauge, Greg McKnight, Mike Judge, Dany Levy, Dave Eggers, Rory Evans, Lisa Birnbach, Nancy Jo Sales, Jessica Anya Blau, and Ariel Kaminer.

And since we've gone over onto the next page, it seems right to honor the *New Yorker* as an institution, for which I've always written, if not always published, and to thank the three editors who allowed me into their legacy—Robert Gottlieb, Tina Brown, and David Remnick, the last of whom I've actually met and who seems nice.

And I might as well acknowledge the writers I've appropriated over the years and cobbled together into something approaching a style: Woody Allen, Robert Benchley, Donald Barthelme, Thomas Pynchon, Michael O'Donohue, Kurt Andersen, et al.

And, finally, I'd like to thank my wife and children, whose adorable antics were the heart and soul of this book, before the edit.

About the Author

Larry Doyle is a freelance journalist living in Chicago. This is his first appearance in the magazine.

•

Larry Doyle is a freelance writer. His article "Eddie Varner Says 'Yes!'(Can You Hear Him?)" appeared in our November issue.

•

Larry Doyle wrote "Cleveland Is Between Here and There," which appeared in these pages last month.

•

"Minneapolis–St. Paul Are What You Would Call Fraternal Twins" and "Nobody Lives in Gary, Indiana, by Choice" are two recent pieces Larry Doyle wrote for this magazine. He has often been sighted in Chicago, where he lives.

•

Larry Doyle's work appears frequently in the magazine. This piece is adapted from "Chicago: City on the Take Out," from the literary dining guide *Red Haute Chicago*, available from the Garlic Press.

•

Larry Doyle's travel pieces for this magazine have been collected into the volume *Within a Day's Drive: Short Trips from Home*, available from Gulf and Western Press for $8.95, or 99 cents with a fill-up at participating stations.

•

Larry Doyle's wry observations on the Midwest and the world can be heard on National Public Radio's *Frequent Modulations*.

•

Larry Doyle is our Heartland Editor. "The Kane County Summerstock Massacre," about his recent foray into playwriting, was awarded the Plimpton Prize.

•

Larry Doyle recently married and moved to Wisconsin. He is at work on a novel.

•

Larry Doyle, whose "Put Another Pecan Log on the Fire: Cheeseheads at Home" in March generated more mail than any article in this magazine's history, reports that he has "returned to the relative civilization of Chicago." He is at work on a novel.

•

Larry Doyle's first novel, *White Guys, Big Shoulders*, will be published by Little Cat Feet Prints in February.

•

Excerpted from Larry Doyle's first novel, *Wise Guys, Big Shoulders,* to be published by Polyhymn Press in October. It has been selected as an alternative selection of the Alternative Book of the Month Club.

•

Larry Doyle is a special senior contributing writer-at-large to the magazine. His first novel, *Bright Guys, Big Shoulders,* is reviewed in this issue.

•

Larry Doyle returns to these pages after a long absence. He is living in Los Angeles and working on a screenplay.

•

Larry Doyle is a Chicagoan in exile. "Milk Chocolate Blondes on Fire," which appeared in this magazine last June, won the Mailer Award for Reportorial Excellence.

•

Larry Doyle is a misplaced midwesterner living in the land of fruit and nuts. The film *Big Shoulders,* starring Robert De Niro and Brad Pitt and scheduled for Christmas release, is based on his novel.

•

Larry Doyle's most recent work for the magazine, "Lights! Camera! Ego!" appeared in November.

•

Bright Guys, starring Rob Schneider and Bruce the Wonder Moose, is available from World Premiere Video. The film is based on Larry Doyle's fotonovella of the same name.

•

Guy Bright is a pseudonym for a well-known midwestern writer residing and earning a living on the West Coast. His wry observations on the film industry will appear from time to time in these pages.

•

Larry Doyle teaches creative writing at the Extension University of Indiana at Gary.

•

Larry Doyle, an associate professor of English, recently published his hypertextual second novel, *Alice Up the Glass Tower,* available in Lotus and Hypercard formats.

•

Alice Up the Glass Tower, Larry Doyle's second novel, is currently in its ninth upgrade.

•

Larry Doyle has a new wife, a new home, and a new novel in the works in Connecticut.

•

Larry Doyle, a regular contributor to the magazine, is currently working on his third novel.

•

Larry Doyle's third novel, currently in revisions, has been hailed as equal to his best work by those who have seen it.

•

Excerpted from Larry Doyle's third novel, an as-yet-untitled work in progress.

•

Larry Doyle recently lost 480 pounds. This piece is adapted from his inspirational vlog, *The Fat Gent Sings.*

•

Longtime readers of this publication may recognize Larry Doyle's byline. For the past seven years he has been working for the U.S. Postal Service, researching a novel.

•

Laurence Eugene Doyle wrote for the print version of this magazine, as well as a number of others. This is excerpted from *Lights Out, Bright Guys!* a novel he was working on at the time of his rampage.